When a Bitch Fed UP

Kevina Hopkins

Dedication

This novel is dedicated to my beautiful children Ashanti and Bakari. You make mommy go above and beyond for you. I love you more than life itself. To my younger siblings Kitiana and Kevin Jr. never give up on whatever it is you want to do in life. No matter how many times you fall get back up. To my guardian angel, Travis Thomas R.I.P, I love and miss you big brother.

Prologue

Mia entered her house through the back door and dropped her keys on the kitchen counter. She stripped down to her underwear in hopes that her husband would be in a good mood by now and give her some loving. She pushed the door open that led to the living room and stopped right in her tracks. She couldn't believe what she was seeing. Her husband was sitting on the couch with his eyes closed and a bitch on her knees in between his legs sucking his dick.

"Seantrel what the fuck is going on in here," Mia yelled!

Seantrel opened his eyes and looked at Mia as if he was pissed off that she had interrupted his nut. The chick that was sucking Seantrel's dick lifted her head up and looked as if her soul had left her body.

Mia stood there frozen in place as her heart pace sped up. She could not believe her eyes. Mia knew that this had to be some kind of sick joke.

Mia instantly felt sick and ran into the kitchen and threw up in the sink.

She had always known about Seantrel's infidelities but she dealt with it because of their kids and he was an excellent provider but this shit took things to another level. She couldn't believe how disrespectful he was being. She was even more hurt by the chick that he decided to fuck in their home.

By the time Seantrel decided to chase after Mia she was stumbling to pull her jeans up as the tears fell from her

5eyes. She couldn't get her clothes fixed fast enough so that she could get out of that house.

Seantrel walked over to Mia and wiped the tears from her eyes.

Mia looked up at Seantrel and gave him a look of disgust. The nigga didn't even have the decency to put his pants back on.

"Don't you ever put your hands on me again in your life?"

Seantrel ignored Mia and reached for her again and before he knew it Mia had slapped the shit out of him.

Seantrel reached his hand up to grab Mia but she grabbed the knife off the counter. He lifted his hands to surrender and exited the kitchen as quickly as he walked in.

Mia grabbed her keys to leave the house but changed her mind. She dropped the keys on the counter and stormed into the living room with the knife. Seantrel had started this game but Mia was going to be the one to end it.

THE BEGINNING

CHAPTER 1

Mia Williams stood in front of her vanity mirror applying her make up when there was a knock at her bedroom door.

"What's up?" Mia called out.

"You ready?" Mianca asked as she pushed the door open

Mia looked up at her beautiful sister and smiled. Mianca had on a Royal blue peplum top, black jeggings, blue wedges, and a blue MK purse to match.

"Why the hell did you knock if you were just going to barge in anyway?"

Mianca ignored her comment and sat on the bed while Mia finished getting dressed.

Mia applied the last of her makeup then turned around to look at her sister.

"How do I look?" Mia asked as she spun around in a circle.

"You look absolutely beautiful."

Mia had on a red and black strapless skater dress that stopped a few inches above her knees with a red pair of 4 inch wedge heels making her stand at almost 5'11 instead of her normal 5'7 frame.

"Thank you," Mia said with a smile as she grabbed her red MK purse and watch off the bed.

Mia and Mianca went down the stairs where everyone was waiting on them at.

"It took y'all long enough," said Mianca's husband Isaiah.

"Now you know you can't rush perfection, besides it's my 21st birthday so I have the right to take my time," said Mia as she playfully punched her brother-in-law.

"Well you look absolutely stunning bff," LaShon said as she hugged Mia.

"Thanks bff, you look beautiful as well."

"Well everyone has said their hellos now let's get out of here," said Mianca.

The group walked outside to the waiting hummer limousine and got inside en-route to club Krush for Mia's birthday party.

They laughed and joked around during the entire ride to the club. Mia loved her small circle that she kept around. It was always just her, Mianca, and LaShon until Mianca got married but she loved her brother-in-law just as much as she loved her sister.

LaShon and Mia had been best friends since they were seven years old. They grew up living right next door to each other and attended the same elementary school, high school, and college. They had their fair share of arguments but that never stopped them from being able to fix their relationship. LaShon was definitely Mia's ride a die and if LaShon was a guy she would have been Mia's future husband. Mia loved LaShon to pieces and wouldn't trade her for the world.

"Hey snap out of it, we're here," said LaShon pushing Mia's arm.

Mia pulled out her compact mirror and applied a little lip gloss before exiting the limousine.

Mia, Mianca, LaShon and Isaiah walked right up to the front of the line and gave their names to enter the club. The hostess checked their ID cards before escorting them to the V.I.P section of the club.

Club Krush was packed and the music was off the chain as usual. There were two sides to the club, a side that was for the wild people and a side for the mellow people. The V.I.P section was upstairs seeing over both sides of the club so they were able to see a view of everything.

LaShon and Mia stood up and danced together to a few of the songs from the loud speakers until someone came and tapped Mia on her shoulder.

Mia turned around and looked at the fine specimen in front of her. He had to be one of the finest men she had ever met in her life. He looked to be about 6'1, light skinned with waves that were so slick that she could get sea sick from looking at them. Not to mention his chiseled chest that peeked out to her from his button up shirt.

"Heeeeyy," Mia slurred. The 5th shot of Ciroc she had finally caught up with her and had her feeling good.

"Hey baby girl, I been watching you from across the room and I couldn't resist coming to speak to you."

"Well, I been watching you watch me," Mia said with a laugh.

The sexy stranger couldn't help but laugh and Mia instantly felt herself get hot. He had the sexiest dimple on the right side of his face that she couldn't resist poking. To Mia's surprise he didn't slap her hand away like a normal person would have. He rubbed his hand over hers instead causing her to snatch her hand away. There was no way that a perfect stranger was supposed to be making her feel that way.

"So sexy lady, what's your name?"

"Mia, what's yours?"

"Seantrel," he said with a smile showing off that gorgeous dimple of his again.

Damn, this man is sexy with a dimple and a sexy ass name. I'm going to have to get his digits she thought.

"That is a very unique and sexy name, but I'm sure you get that a lot," Mia said flirting.

"Thank you, I do get that a lot but not from someone as beautiful as you."

"You are such a charmer, you better watch out before I cuff you," Mia said half jokingly.

"Well don't you need my number before you bring out the cuffs," asked Seantrel?

"Hold on let me grab my phone off the table."

Mia walked over to where her sister was sitting at and snatched her phone off the table. She gave Mianca a look that said "don't say anything."
Mia unlocked her phone then handed it to Seantrel so that he could store his phone number. Instead of him saving the number he called his own phone from her phone and then allowed Mia to save it herself.

While Mia started typing in Seantrel's name "Wetter" by: Twista came on and Mia started her deadly slow wind. She moved her body and hips hypnotizing any man that was looking her way. Seantrel stood looking at her for about a minute lost in a trance before he walked up on her and grabbed her by the hips allowing her body to rub up against his rock hard body and manhood.

Seantrel wanted so badly to caress Mia's body but he opted on keeping his hands in a respectable place.

Mia could feel Seantrel's manhood start to grow as she rubbed her ass on him. She couldn't help but smile, it showed her that she still got it and it showed her that he was working with something very nice in his jeans.

Mia and Seantrel danced together for a couple more songs as if they were the only people in the club. Mia was so into the music and Seantrel that she closed her eyes and allowed his hands to roam over her body.

Mianca sat watching her sister dance until she saw Seantrel's hands go a little bit too far up Mia's dress. That's when she knew it was time to break them up. Mianca was all for Mia having fun but being that she had liquor in her system she was capable of allowing anything to happen.

Mianca stood to go stop her sister but Isaiah grabbed her wrist to stop her.

"Don't do it, it's her birthday, she's grown and just having fun."

Mianca was about to reply to Isaiah until she saw Mia walking towards her.

"Hey y'all, this is my new handsome friend Seantrel."

"Hey," Seantrel said.

"Hey," everyone said in unison.

Mia and Seantrel sat in the corner and kicked it with each other. They laughed and joked around and danced to the music some more. Before they knew it time had flew by and it was 3:30 in the morning.

Mia was tempted to leave the club with Seantrel but she knew that would only lead to sex. She wanted to actually get to know the sexy man and sleeping with him on the first night that she met him would not be a good idea so she gave him a hug and a kiss on the cheek before leaving the club with her family.

She was on her way home hot and bothered yet again. It had been almost five months since the last time she had sex and her B.O.B was no longer scratching the itch. Just the thought of it made her mad at her boyfriend Dante all over again for getting locked up. She had been celibate all this time trying to wait on him but she was getting tired of the wait and the way Dante's case was going it was no telling when he was coming home so now it was time for her to do her.

CHAPTER 2

Mia walked into her bedroom and stripped down to nothing but her panties. She grabbed her makeup removal and cleansed her face thoroughly before tossing the pad into the garbage.

Mia turned off her bedroom lights and then climbed in bed and got under her sheets. She closed her eyes and tried to sleep but she couldn't help but toss and turn. She was horny and Seantrel's sexy smile kept popping up in her head.

Mia reached over into her nightstand drawer and took out her bullet. She closed her eyes and opened her legs. She thought about the things that she wanted Seantrel to do to her body and begin to rub her clit slowly. She could imagine his lips licking her body from head to toe. She could feel him biting soft hickeys on her neck and then her collarbone. She arched her back and allowed a soft moan escape her lips. She kept rubbing her clit softly imaging that Seantrel's lips was the bullet.

Mia felt her body tense up and shake and knew that she was on the verge of cumming. She rubbed a little faster until she felt her juices slide down her hands. "Damn," Mia said out loud.

The orgasm helped Mia relax some but it only left her wanting more. The only thing that would truly satisfy her now would be a stiff dick.

Mia wiped her bullet off with a baby wipe that was on her nightstand and placed it back in her drawer before closing her eyes and drifting off to sleep.

Mia could hear her cell phone ringing and kicked herself for not turning it off. It was only 8:00 in the morning and she wondered who the hell was calling her phone so early in the morning on a Sunday. Everyone knew that if it wasn't an emergency not to call her before noon.

Mia reached over and grabbed her phone and saw that it was Seantrel calling. She sat up and rubbed her hair down as if he could see her through the phone.

"Hello," Mia answered.

"Hey, did I wake you?"

"No, I was just getting up," she lied.

"I was wondering if I could take you out to brunch."

Mia was surprised that Seantrel had called already and for a date at that but that wasn't going to stop her from accepting his invitation.

"Yes, I'll go out with you."

"Well I can pick you up or you can meet up with me, whichever one makes you more comfortable."

Mia thought about it for a minute before responding.

"I actually have a couple of runs to make so how about I just meet you somewhere around 1 o'clock."

"Ok cool, we can go anywhere you want to go. Just text me the place at least an hour before so that I can meet you," said Seantrel.

"Alright, sounds like a plan," Mia said before hanging up her phone.

Mia laid back down and closed her eyes and tried to go back to sleep for at least another hour but it was no use so she got up and looked for something to put on for the day.

Mia grabbed a white sundress out of her closet and a pair of white wedge heels to match. She took out her black panties and black strapless bra to go under her dress. By the time Mia finished getting dressed and combing her hair it was already 9:30.

Mia grabbed her purse and went downstairs to the kitchen to grab a blueberry muffin to go. As soon as she opened the kitchen door she saw Isaiah standing at the refrigerator in nothing but his boxers.

"My bad Mia, I didn't think you would be up so early," said Isaiah trying to cover himself up.

"It's cool, I didn't plan on being up this early either but I have some errands to go run so tell Mianca to call my phone if she needs me."

Mia walked over to the cabinet and grabbed a muffin and orange juice from the refrigerator before exiting the house.

Mia walked outside and got in her red 2004 Nissan Sentra. She turned the radio on and headed to her mother's house lost in her thoughts. She was on a total emotional rollercoaster and hoped that this visit didn't end in a screaming match between her and her step father as usual.

Mia pulled up in front of her mother's apartment complex and breathed a sigh of relief when she didn't see her step father's car outside. She knocked on the door and her mother swung it open without even seeing who it was first.

"Hey ma," Mia said with a look of disgust on her face.

"Hey, and don't you even start it with me. It's too early for your shit."

Mia was shocked by her mother's words but she shouldn't have expected anything less. She no longer knew who her mother was. Her mother hadn't been herself for the last past three years and it seemed like every time Mia came to check on her she was getting worse.

Mia thought about the time when Melissa was once a very beautiful woman with a nice shape, bubbly attitude and loving heart. She would have given the world for her children at one point but one day she just began to change unexpectedly. She started staying away from home days at a time and would return in the same clothes she had on when she left only they were filthy. Mia's father figured out that his wife had a drug habit and he tried to hide it from his children and get her some help but it didn't work.

Mr. Jackson eventually gave up hope and moved out hoping that would push Melissa to get her shit together faster. Mia was only 18 years old at the time and Mianca was 21 years old but she had already moved out. Mr. Jackson went and found a condo for himself and bought a house that he felt both Mia and Mianca should live in together. He believed that they were both responsible enough to maintain a house.

Mia and Mianca were determined not to end up like their mother and wanted to prove to their father that he had made the right decision so they both went to school and found jobs to take care of themselves. Their father helped pay the bills at the house up until Mianca married Isaiah but even then he gave Mia money and helped her with her expenses.

Melissa seemed to not care much though because not even a month after her family moved out she moved Angelo in. Mia hated Angelo from the first time she saw him and she hated the way he looked at her. He gave her a look that always made her feel uncomfortable and like he was undressing her with his eyes. She told her mother about it once but her mother tried to blame it on her and said it was because of the way she dressed that was causing her to get his attention. After that day Mia tried her best to avoid going to see her mother while Angelo was around. Then to make matters worse as soon as Melissa and Robert's divorce was finalized she went and married Angelo.

Mia shook her head to clear those thoughts away before looking up at her frail mother standing in front of her.

"Ma, I didn't come over to get in a fight. I just wanted to come and check on you."

"Check on me for what? I'm fine, can't you tell," Melissa asked while swinging her frail arms in the air.

Mia looked around the filthy living room that had trash and dishes all over it. There were even small baggies on the table that still had crack rock residue in them.

The sight made Mia vomit in her mouth.

"Ma, are you serious? This is no way for anyone to live. Why don't you let me go take you to get your hair done and buy you some clothes?"

"I don't need you to do any of that. You can just give me the money and I'll take myself."

"You and I both know what you will do with the money if I give it to you. I have no problem helping you out financially but I am not about to support your habit."

Melissa was about to respond to Mia until her husband rushed into the house like someone was after him.

Mia turned around and looked at Angelo as he charged at Melissa and smacked the taste out of her mouth.

"Didn't I tell your ass no one was allowed in my house while I was gone?"

He lifted his hand to swing on Melissa again but Mia grabbed it.

"You can do whatever the fuck you want to do with my mother when I'm not here but I won't stand here and allow you to beat her ass in front of me."

Angelo looked down at his arm and then back up at Mia's face and gave her a toothless smile.

Mia released his arm and stepped back. His breath and body reeked of alcohol and piss.

"Would you like to take her place then," asked Angelo?

"Nigga if you ever put your hands on me you must not ever want to use them again because they will be chopped the fuck off," said Mia with a straight face.

Angelo looked at Mia and knew that she was serious so he retracted his attention back to Melissa.

"You just gone let this little bitch stand here and talk to me like that?"

17

Before Angelo knew what was happening Mia had her hands around his thin neck trying to choke the life out of him.

Melissa rushed over and pulled Mia off of him.

"What the hell are you doing? You're going to kill him. He didn't mean any harm," she cried.

"Ma, you disgust me, you can tolerate his bullshit but I don't have to. I'm not married to his ass."

"I want her out of my house now," Angelo yelled!

"Mia I think its best that you leave. I will give you a call later on today."

Mia was to hurt to even speak so she turned around and walked out the house not even bothering to close the door.

As soon as Mia got in her car and pulled off she broke down and cried. She didn't know why she subjected herself to the bullshit. Mianca had been given up on their mother and had been telling Mia for the past year that nothing was going to change about their mother's situation. Mianca tried to convince Mia to let it go and stop visiting but the love that Mia had for her mother wouldn't allow it to happen.

Mia knew that she couldn't call and tell her sister or father what had just taken place or things would only get worse. She never shared the events that happened when she visited because as far as they knew she had stopped going to see Melissa so she always carried the burden on her shoulders.

CHAPTER 3

Mia pulled up into Forest home cemetery and drove around to the gravesite that she was looking for. She parked and took a deep breath before getting out of the car. She grabbed the flowers that she bought and the blanket that she always kept in her car. Mia closed her car door and walked around until she found the headstone that she was looking for. She placed the flowers on the headstone and then placed the blanket on the ground as she read the inscription written on the headstone.

Maurice Jackson

March 18, 1984- October 15, 2010

Loving son, brother and friend

Gone but never forgotten

A single tear dropped from Mia's eyes as she rubbed her hands across the words. She sat down on the ground and began to have a conversation with her brother as if he could respond to her.

"Hey big head, I've been missing you like crazy. Yesterday was my birthday and you know I partied to the max. I just wish you were there to celebrate with me. Things haven't been the same since you left us. Mommy hasn't made any progress and it doesn't seem like she's attempting to. I talked to daddy yesterday and he seems to be doing well. I'm going to go to Kentucky in the next couple of weeks to check on him myself. You know he is always trying to play strong. Mianca and Isaiah are doing great but I think it's time for me to get ready and move out and get my own place. And before you protest I'm 21 years old now and Mianca and Isaiah need their own space."

Mia paused for emphasis as she gave it some more thought. It really was time for her to move on and figure out what it really was that she wanted out of life.

Mia sat and talked with Maurice for a little while longer and closed her eyes as her thoughts begun to drift off to the day he passed away. It was a day that she would never forget. She remembered it like it was yesterday instead of eight months ago. She had nightmares about it every time she closed her eyes for the first couple of weeks after his death.

Mia had just left the house and needed to stop at the gas station before going to work. As she was pumping her gas she got a call from her brother's girlfriend.

"Hello," Mia answered.

"Mia you have to hurry up and get to the hospital. It's Maurice and it's not looking good."

"Hold on what do you mean it's not looking good? I just talked to him last week and everything was fine," Mia yelled into the phone.

"Maurice got into a fight a couple days ago and one of the boys hit him in the head with a bat. He was rushed to the hospital then but was released but now he's back in there and he had a seizure this morning and one of the arteries in his brain cracked. The doctors don't expect him to make it through the night," Chanel said.

Mia paused not believing what she was hearing. She had just talked to her brother and no one had even called her and informed her or Mianca that something had happened to him in the first place.

"What hospital is he at?"

"He's at U.I.C. hospital."

Mia hung up the phone not even bothering to respond. She immediately dialed Mianca's number and fought back the tears that were threatening to drop. As soon as Mianca answered Mia broke down and cried barely able to explain to her sister what Chanel told her. By the time Mia finished telling Mianca what happened Mianca was storming out the house with Isaiah right behind her.

Mia didn't realize she was still standing at the gas pump aimlessly until someone started blowing their horn for the pump.

Mia placed the pump back and closed the nozzle on her car and stormed to the hospital like a bat out of hell. As soon as she went into the hospital she gave her brother's name and was given a visitor's pass.

Mia stood at the elevator pressing the button as if it would make the elevator move faster. She pressed the button for the 4th floor and prayed during the entire time of the ride. She rushed to Maurice's hospital room and immediately stopped where she stood. She could barely recognize her brother with all of the bandages wrapped around his head and the swelling of his body.

"Is he in a coma?" Mia asked the nurse as she choked on her words.

"No he isn't, this is just his current state right now," the nurse said.

"What do you mean his current state? Are you saying my brother is a vegetable," Mia asked confused?

The nurse gave Mia a sad look before saying, "I'll have his doctor come and talk to you soon."

Mia nodded her head and sat on the couch that was in the room as the nurse made her exit. Mia felt like she was losing a part of herself as she watched her brother lay there helplessly. He wasn't breathing on his own and his blood was being washed in and out of his body like they did a patient that was on dialysis. That was the first time ever in her 20 years of life that she had ever seen her brother so weak.

Mia pulled out her phone and called Mianca.

"Yeah," Mianca answered.

"I'm at the hospital and it's not looking good. I know you're not going to want to do this but you have to go get mama. I already sent daddy a text and told him to come to the hospital."

"I'm already on it, I'm pulling up to this dump that she calls a house now. I'll see you in a few minutes."

"Alright, hurry up," Mia said before hanging up.

Mia managed to stand up and walked over to her brother. She rubbed the side of his face as the tears cascaded from her eyes. She never had felt so much pain in her entire life. She kissed Maurice and whispered "I love you," in his ear.

Mia exited the room and went to find the waiting room that was for them. Mia walked into the room and saw Chanel with her mother and brother.

"What is going on Chanel? Why am I just getting a call from you today? My brother chart says that he's been in here for three days."

"Mia we wanted to call you, I swear but Maurice said he didn't want to worry you and Mianca. We tried not to call you but after they resuscitated him earlier and said that they needed to talk to his immediate family I had no choice but to call you."

Mia looked at Chanel like she was crazy. That had to be one of the dumbest things she had ever heard before. If it hadn't have been for Chanel's family sitting in there she would have slapped the shit out of her.

Mia sat in the waiting room until Mianca, Isaiah, her mother and father entered the room. She immediately hopped up and hugged her father and broke down. She let out all the pain that she had been holding in. She used her father as her rock and protector. Mr. Jackson just stood there and rubbed Mia's back as he fought back tears of his own.

Once everyone seemed to calm down the doctor entered the room to talk to the family. She informed the family that she didn't believe Maurice would make it through the night. They could either allow him to suffer or pull the plug right now. There was no way that anyone was going to agree on pulling the plug so they sat in the waiting area quietly. Each of them took turns going back and forth to Maurice hospital room. No one had any words to say to each other. They were all having their own turmoil's with the situation.

Not even two hours after the doctor had spoken to the family Mianca was running back to the waiting area saying something was wrong. Everyone immediately ran out of the waiting room towards Maurice's hospital room. They watched as Maurice room filled up with nurses, doctors, and student doctors. They each took turns performing CPR on him. Mia felt weak in the knees and instantly dropped to the floor. Her father lifted her up and held her tightly in his arms. She could hear Mianca screaming in the background telling the doctor's "stop, you're hurting him. Stop you're hurting him," she cried out even more.

Mia snatched away from her father and went and stood with her sister and held onto her tightly as they cried together. Even though the doctors continued to perform CPR Mia knew that Maurice was gone. The doctors were applying so much pressure to his chest compressions that the bed was bouncing up and down.

Mr. Jackson could no longer bear to watch them work on his son any longer so he just told the doctors to stop. They had already been trying for seven minutes and nothing was changing. Mia cried even harder and let out a gut wrenching scream. She didn't know what hurt her worse, watching her brother suffer or watching him die.

Mia had finally calmed down but her mother had her puzzled. She didn't see her mother shed a single tear or try to sooth her or Mianca's pain. She didn't even get as much as a hug from her. If Mia knew any better she would have did like Mianca and her father and washed her hands of her mother.

Mia felt the vibrating of her phone and opened her eyes. She wiped the tears from her eyes and pulled out her phone to see who was calling. She looked at the screen and saw that it was Seantrel. "Damn," Mia said before answering her phone.

"Hello!"

"Let me find out you trying to stand me up already," Seantrel said in his panty dropping voice.

"I am so sorry, I lost track of time. We can meet at the Denny's on Harlem and North Ave at 1'oclock still if you have enough time," Mia said hoping he didn't change his mind.

"It's cool baby girl, I'll see you in an hour."

Mia gave a sigh of relief as she hung up her phone. She hadn't realized that she had been sitting there lost in her thoughts for almost an hour.

Mia stood up and pulled her dress all the way down then folded up her blanket.

"I love you big brother, I have a lunch date with this guy I just met. Hopefully he's a keeper then I can tell you about him my next visit," Mia said with a smile before walking towards her car.

Mia placed the blanket in the trunk and then entered the car and started it. She gave a sigh of relief. Although she could not get use to her big brother being gone it was becoming a little easier for her because at one point she didn't even know how she was going to survive life without him. She was at the point in her life that she just had to take everything one day at a time and try to keep a piece of mind.

CHAPTER 4

Mia made it to Denny's 15 minutes early so she went in the restroom and cleaned her face and reapplied her makeup. By the time she finished her skin was flawless and you never would have known she was just crying 30 minutes ago.

Mia walked out to find a table and almost walked right past Seantrel until he grabbed her by the arm.

"Hey beautiful, you forgot what I look like already?" Seantrel asked with a smile.

That man's smile was definitely contagious because all Mia could do was return the smile before taking a seat.

"I'm sorry about that, I wasn't even paying attention."

"It's cool, I was just about to text you and tell you where I was seated but I see you beat me here."

"Yeah, I was at the cemetery," Mia said before lowering her head slightly.

Seantrel could see the sadness wipe across Mia's face so decided to change the subject and not pry.

"So did you dream about me last night," asked Seantrel?

Mia looked up and laughed, "We're a little full of ourselves aren't we?"

"What? I dreamed about you last night, that's why you were the first person I called this morning," Seantrel said truthfully.

Mia couldn't help but blush and that's when she got a good look at Seantrel. The club did him no justice, he was sexier then she remembered. He had the most greenish/ hazel eyes she had ever seen. He had to be mixed with something and she couldn't resist asking.

"Are you mixed with something?"

"Yes, my mama and my daddy," he said jokingly.

"Ha, ha, ha smart ass."

"Nah but for real, I am mixed though, my dad is black and my mom is Puerto Rican and black. Her father was Puerto Rican and her mother was black."

"Cool, well that's one sexy combination."

The waiter came over and took Seantrel and Mia's order before they continued their conversation.

"Thank you beautiful, so tell me about you," said Seantrel.

"Well yesterday was my 21st birthday and I'm the youngest of three kids. I have an older sister and an older brother well had an older brother, he passed away October of last year. My sister Mianca and I have been living together for the past 3 years. I work for a collection agency and go to Chicago State University."

"I like that, a young lady who's trying to get somewhere in life."

"Yes sir, I wouldn't have it any other way now it's your turn to tell me something about you."

"I just made 26 on the 22nd of last month. I'm single with no kids. I have a brother named Steven who's 21 years old and a sister named Stephanie who's 27 years old. I don't depend on anyone for anything and I live on my own. I like to cook and please my woman. I have a legit job, well actually two. I work for Ford and I'm in the process of starting my own landscaping company."

The waitress brought Mia and Seantrel their food and kept it moving. As soon as she left they begin to eat and Seantrel continued to tell Mia about his life. Mia listened in awe because the man sitting in front of her seemed too good to be true and from where she came from they tended to be too good then. There was no such thing as the perfect man in Mia's eyes.

Seantrel actually told Mia more about himself then she did about herself. He went into details about his family and she was happy that he was raised in a two parent home and his parents were still together. That rarely happened so she loved to see couples still together after all those years of marriage.

"So what do you have planned for the rest of the day," Mia asked?

"My day is free so hopefully I can spend some more time with you."

"That sounds like a plan to me."

"Alright then, let me pay the bill then we can get out of here," said Seantrel.

Mia and Seantrel spent the remainder of the day downtown at Navy Pier, walking and talking. Mia opened up a little more with Seantrel but she left out the part about her mother being on drugs.

Mia and Seantrel stopped at Daminzeo's and grabbed a pizza before Mia followed Seantrel back to his house. Mia was impressed with the neighborhood that Seantrel lived in. It was a nice secluded area in Indiana.

Mia parked her car on the side of his in the driveway before he led her into his house. Mia walked in and admired the furniture and pictures on the wall.

"Make yourself comfortable, I'm going to get some plates and something for us to drink."

Mia immediately slipped out of her wedge toe heels. Her feet had been kicking her ass all day but she wanted to stay cute and not switch to her flip flops.

"Come let me take you on a tour of the house," Seantrel said as he grabbed Mia by the hand.

Seantrel showed Mia every room of the house and by the time she made it by the living room she was definitely convinced that it had to be something going on with Seantrel. This man had a job, no kids, no girlfriend, great taste and a four bedroom 2 story house that was almost cleaner then hers. He was the man that she always said she wanted but knew that she would never find.

"Your house is beautiful," Mia said as she sat down." Did you decorate it yourself?"
"I would love to take the credit for this but my mom and one of my home girls did it for me."

"That's what's up."

Mia and Seantrel started a movie and ate. Mia relaxed as Seantrel placed his muscular arm around her. She felt like she was on the verge of melting. She couldn't take sitting this close to him and not doing anything. Before Mia knew it she was straddling Seantrel's lap and placing soft kisses on his neck and collar bone.

Seantrel lifted Mia's head and placed a gentle kiss on Mia's mouth before their tongues hungrily found each other. Mia tried to reason with herself, her mind was telling her to stop but her body was saying to go for it.

Mia stopped for air and pulled Seantrel's tank top over his head. She admired the cross tattoo that was on his chest and kissed it as she rubbed her hand up and down his rock hard abs.

Seantrel placed his hands up under Mia's dress and played with the rim of her boy shorts before placing his thick fingers down her underwear and finding her clit. He twirled his finger around it until Mia began to tremble. He didn't want to waste a good nut with his finger so he lifted her up and laid her down on her back.

Seantrel pulled Mia's underwear down and pulled her dress off. He sat there and admired her body first. She had some of the smoothest skin and he couldn't find not one flaw or stretch mark on it.

Mia smiled as she saw Seantrel admire her body. She knew that she kept her shit right and made sure that she stayed in the gym so she was never hesitant or ashamed about taking her clothes off in front of anyone. Mia had a body that a lot of grown women would kill for.

Seantrel stuck his head in between Mia's legs and inhaled her sent before diving in head first. He twirled his tongue around her clit then licked the insides of her lips. He placed two of his fingers inside of her vagina and moved them in and out.

"Ahhhhh," Mia moaned out in ecstasy. Seantrel definitely knew what he was doing on the oral side. If his dick was as good as his head she was going to have to get her handcuffs and cuff the nigga for real.

Seantrel pursed his lips together and hummed on Mia's pearl tongue.

Mia wrapped her thighs tightly around Seantrel's neck as her body started to tremble.

Seantrel continued to suck until Mia's body stopped jerking. Once she seemed like she had calmed down he stripped out of all his clothes and his 9 ½ inch dick stood at attention. He reached down into his pants and grabbed a condom and put it on. Before Mia could protest or say anything Seantrel was at her wet opening gently putting his dick inside of her.

Seantrel gently moved in and out of Mia and pressed on her clit with his thumb gently.

"Damn, Seantrel, what the hell," Mia managed to say.

Seantrel was stroking Mia so good that she began to dig her fingers into his back.

"Ooohh daddy, right there, push a little harder."

Seantrel lifted Mia's leg in the crook of his arm and plunged faster and harder causing Mia to bust all on his dick.

Seantrel pulled out and flipped Mia on her stomach. It was now his turn to get his nut off.

Seantrel dug deeper and it felt like Mia could feel him in her stomach.

Seantrel begin to groan and Mia threw her pussy back at him. She knew it was only a matter of time before he busted and she wanted to cum one more time before he did.

"Cum on daddy, cum with me," Mia purred.

Seantrel placed a kiss on Mia's back right before he released his nut into the condom.

"Where have you been all my life," Mia uttered before kissing Seantrel on his lips.

Seantrel helped Mia up off the couch so that they could take a shower and then finish watching the movie that they started.

Seantrel and Mia watched the movie for a little while before they passed out on the couch.

CHAPTER 5

Mianca looked up at the clock that read 10:00 A.M. as she paced back and forth across the living room floor with her phone in her hands. She had been calling Mia's phone since last night and it had been going straight to voicemail. She had even called LaShon's phone to see was Mia with her but LaShon said that she hadn't heard from Mia since they left her party. In fact LaShon had been texting and calling Mia since 8:00 last night.

"Baby will you sit down and relax. I'm sure everything is fine with Mia," said Isaiah.

"Isaiah how can you tell me to relax when I haven't gotten so much as a hello from my sister yesterday and now she isn't even answering her phone. We both know that she's more responsible than this and wouldn't stay out without letting us know.

"Mia isn't," Isaiah started but stopped once he heard the kitchen sliding door open.

Mianca rushed for the kitchen before Isaiah could stop her.

"Where the hell have you been?" Mianca immediately asked.

"Hello to you too," Mia said with an attitude before walking pass Mianca and going in the living room.

Mianca grabbed Mia by her arm and spun her around.

"What the hell is your problem Mianca? And get your hands off of me, I'm not your child," Mia screamed as she snatched her arm away.

"Maybe you two need to just calm down," Isaiah said being the peace maker.

"I don't need to calm down. You need to tell your wife that," Mia said never taking her attention away from Mianca.

Mianca took a deep breath to calm down before she said something to Mia that she would regret later.

"Look, I'm sorry for grabbing you but you could have at least called me and said you weren't coming home. I haven't had a wink of sleep because I was worried crazy about you. I understand that you're grown now but you have to be more responsible and pick up the phone."

"I'm sorry that you were worried but I lost track of time and fell asleep. By the time I woke up it was after three and my battery was dead so I went back to sleep."

Mianca wanted to ask Mia where did she sleep at last night but knew how her sister's temper could get and decided to save it for a later conversation.

Mia gave Mianca a hug then ran upstairs to her bedroom. She put her phone on the charger then went into her bathroom and took a hot shower. She thought about the hot steamy sex that she and Seantrel had throughout the night and the thought of how he ate her pussy made her clit jump and sent chills up and down her spine.

Mia finished showering and put her robe on before walking back inside of her bedroom. She rubbed lotion on her body before putting on a pair of leggings and a t-shirt. Mia planned on doing the same thing she did every Sunday and that was relax with her laptop and get some much needed studying and homework out of the way.

Mia powered her phone on and pulled out her laptop so that she could check her emails and start on her Psychology homework. Mia had one more year to go then she'd have her bachelor's degree in Social Work. She worked hard over the years and made sure that she didn't allow anything that went on in her personal life to deter her from her education.

Mia was halfway in the middle of reading a chapter when her phone vibrated on the nightstand. She looked over at the phone and saw who it was. She debated on if she wanted to answer it or not.

"Hello," Mia said into the phone.

"Damn, you don't sound too happy to hear from me."

"Hey Dante, how are you doing?" Mia asked in a fake chipper voice.

"I'm doing as well as I can be in this situation."

Mia took a deep breath and closed her laptop. She knew this was about to be another pity party conversation.

"Can we please not go down that road? We have this conversation every time until our time runs out on the phone," Mia said slightly annoyed.

Dante chuckled to himself before speaking back into the phone.

"You right, we don't have to have that conversation. How about we talk about this new nigga that you with now?"

"What?" Mia asked thrown back by his question.

"You heard exactly what I said."

"What you got somebody following me now," Mia asked angrily?

"Baby the streets talk and I know your every mood. I commend you on being true to me for the past six months. But let me tell you one damn thing. You can have your fun now but as soon as I get home that nigga better be gone. I invested too much motherfucking time in you and our relationship."

Mia was about to say something before she heard the phone slam into her ear indicating that Dante had hung up the phone on her. She placed the phone back on her night stand and laid her head against the headboard lost in her thoughts no longer being able to concentrate on her homework.

Mia picked her phone back up and called LaShon.

"Hello," LaShon answered.

"Damn girl, did you let the phone ring first," Mia joked.

"Girl whatever, your sister is heated, she been calling my phone all night."

"It's all good, I'm at home now. What's going on with you," asked Mia.

"Nothing, in the house bored."

Mia sighed into the phone, "I can really use my best friend right now."

LaShon couldn't help but smile at Mia's words. Mia was the only person that could get her to get dressed and leave her house just to talk.

"Give me 30 minutes then I'll be there."

"I love you," Mia said into the phone.

"Yeah, yeah, yeah, I love you too. I just hope you got something for me to eat while I'm there."

Mia hung up the phone and went down the stairs into the kitchen so that she could see what snacks were down there for LaShon. She wasn't really hungry because Seantrel had cooked breakfast for her this morning.

Mia looked through the cabinet and found some fig bars, Kellogg's cracker chips and placed them on the counter then went into the refrigerator and grabbed a couple of green teas and placed them on the counter as well before grabbing some napkins.

Isaiah walked into the kitchen as Mia was getting ready to walk out.

"If you that hungry I can fix you something for lunch," Isaiah said seriously.

Mia looked down at the junk food in her arms and laughed.

"All of this isn't for me; actually half of it isn't for me. LaShon is on her way over."

"Awe okay, then that explains a lot. I have never seen anyone that small eat so much food in my life."

LaShon had to be about 125 pounds soaking wet but could eat you out of a house and a home.

"Yeah she sure can, I can't even eat half the food she eats without worrying about losing my figure," Mia said.

"Are you alright now though?" Isaiah asked referring to the incident between her and Mianca earlier.

"Yeah I'm good; I know she didn't mean any harm."

"Alright just go and relax. I'll open the door for LaShon when she gets here," Isaiah said before going in the freezer to take something out for dinner.

Mia went upstairs to her bedroom and placed the junk food on her dresser and grabbed one of the green teas before lying across her bed. Mia laid there and had dozed off before she knew it. She only had about three hours of sleep put together for the entire night. So she was more tired than she realized.

CHAPTER 6

Mia jumped from her bed when she felt someone shaking her arm.

"Girl would your ass relax. What the hell you so jumpy for," asked LaShon.

"Because I felt someone shaking me out of my sleep," Mia said while looking over at the clock. "And your damn 30 minutes was over with almost an hour ago."

"I know and I'm sorry, I was on my way out the door and then my mama wanted me to do something for her."

"It's all good, you're here now."

Mia picked up her phone and saw a missed call and text from Seantrel. She dialed his number and waited for him to answer.

"Hey beautiful," Seantrel said into the phone.

"Hey handsome," Mia replied.

Mia could picture Seantrel's sexy smile with his one dimple in it as she talked to him on the phone.

"What's on your agenda for the rest of the day," he asked.

"Nothing really, homework and hanging with LaShon at my house."

"Well gone ahead and kick it with your home girl and just call me when she leaves. Maybe I can pick you up and take you to get some ice cream."

"Ok, cool, that sounds like a plan to me," Mia said before hanging up.

"Excuse me; who was that you were on the phone with? That nigga got you showing all 32 pearly whites," LaShon said.

"That's what I needed you to come over for so that we could talk. That was Seantrel, you know the sexy brother from the club the other day."

"Of course I remember who could forget a face like his?"

Mia went on to explain the events that took place last night up until the conversation with Dante. She left out the main details of the sex between her and Seantrel. She just told her that they had slept together. Mia loved LaShon like she loved her own sister but it was one thing that she was taught and that was to never share the intimate details about a man as far as sex with another woman because she might get curious enough and want it for herself. Mia had seen it happen so many times that she lost count. So she was thankful that her mother was able to instill that into her before she went on her crack binge.

"Baby girl what seems to be the problem though," asked LaShon in a serious tone? LaShon honestly didn't find anything wrong with what Mia was doing or her situation.

"LaShon I don't know what to do. I mean it's like I still have love for Dante, we have almost 3 years of history and time invested in each other. But on the other hand I'm really feeling Seantrel and wouldn't mind seeing where things could go between us."

"Mia, listen to me and listen to me good because I only want to have this talk with you once. What you and

40

Dante have is puppy love. You're too good for a thug that just wants to sell drugs. I been telling you for the longest that you need to know your worth. Seantrel sounds like a good dude so far from what you're telling me and plus he's a man on his grown man shit and that's what you need. Someone that's equal to your drive and near your pay grade. You don't have to worry about will you be on the phone with him one day and the next day in the visiting room at Cook County Jail."

Mia listened as her best friend talked and was thankful to have her in her life. LaShon was wiser then Mia when it came to some things as far as relationships and the streets even though she was only a few months older than her.

Mia and LaShon were the opposite in a lot of ways but that's what made them so much closer because what LaShon was weak in Mia was strong in and vice versa. Even though Mia's mother was a drug abuser and she moved out at the age of 18 her life was still sheltered. Her mother never abused her or did drugs around her and her father and brother made sure that she never wanted or needed anything. If she ever had any problems she would just run to her dad or older siblings and they would solve the problem for her. Mia worked because she wanted to not because she had to and as far as relationships she only had a couple of boyfriends before Dante but they were just childish high school relationships.

On the other hand LaShon grew up in a single parent home with just her mother and was forced to get a job in order to pay the other half of her tuition. Her mother barely had enough money to keep a roof over their heads and food on their table. When they were younger Mia use to buy clothes for LaShon so that she wouldn't get picked on in school. Once they were in their sophomore year of high school LaShon started dating guys that she knew would be able to buy things for her so that she wouldn't have to depend on Mia anymore. By the time they graduated high school LaShon was labeled a hoe and she was tired of it so she decided to use her brain and go find a job instead of depending on what was between her legs. It was by the grace of God that she had never contracted any kind of disease. Since then LaShon has been working a 9-5 and living with her mother.

LaShon really wanted to move out on her own but she was afraid that if she left her mother wouldn't be able to survive or afford to pay the bills. Mia always convinced her that if that was the case then her mother needed to move into something smaller that she could afford since it would only be her. She always told LaShon that she needed to live her life which was one of the reasons that Mia was going to move out of the house that she shared with her sister. She felt like Mianca wanted to control her and watch her every move like she was her baby sitter.

"Mia, are you listening to what I'm saying," asked LaShon.

"Yes I'm listening and I understand exactly what you're saying. It's time for me to make some changes and live my life."

"So what are you going to do first?"

"I'm going to continue to see Seantrel and see where that goes and in the process start looking for me my own place."

"What about Dante?"

"What about him? Nobody told him to play P.I. once he gets home then we'll cross that bridge. He did say do me so hopefully his people will see me happy and let him know that then he'll move on with his life."

LaShon knew that there was no way that was going to happen. She had dealt with her fair share of jail relationships and every time the dude came home he expected to pick up things where they left off at as if nothing ever happened.

"Alright ma, just be careful," were the only words that LaShon said. She knew once Mia made up her mind there was no reasoning with her.

LaShon grabbed the chips off the dresser and turned on the TV to find something to watch while Mia opened her laptop back up to do some more homework.

"Girl I don't know why you taking summer classes. You are young and supposed to be enjoying your summer to the fullest. Who the hell works during the summer? We both are sexy and have money; we should be on somebody's beach somewhere right about now."

"I already told you, if I take these two classes then I can graduate a semester early. Plus I work during the summer because I have those things called bills."

"Whatever, we both know you don't have to pay any bills around here if you didn't want to."

"I know I don't but I want to show that I'm independent enough to make it on my own. But gone ahead and plan a vacation for the first week of August. Anywhere of your choice and I'm there."

"Yayyyy," LaShon sung as she bounced up and down on Mia's bed.

"Girl if you don't sit your ass down somewhere. You gone have me sleeping on the floor," Mia said playfully pushing LaShon off of her.

Mia studied for a little while longer then closed her laptop and kept LaShon company. Before they knew it Mianca was knocking on the door letting them know dinner was ready.

Mia and LaShon went down stairs to get their food then went right back to Mia's room. Mianca had cooked a pot roast, potatoes, carrots and had Hawaiian rolls. They ate and talked until almost 9:00 and that's when LaShon decided to leave because she knew Mia wanted to hang out with Seantrel for a little while and they had to be up early tomorrow for work.

"I'm driving tomorrow or you," LaShon asked as Mia walked her to the door.

"I'll drive tomorrow so be ready at seven chick."

"Alright see you then."

Mia closed the front door then went upstairs and called Seantrel. She told him that LaShon was gone and she gave him her address so that he could come pick her up. They went to Baskin Robbins up the street and Seantrel got Mia her ice-cream just like he promised her.

CHAPTER 7

Six months had passed and Mia and Seantrel's relationship had been going great. Mia had no complaints towards Seantrel. He had been the same loving and caring man he was when she first met him. He was still taking her out on dates and the sex was still the bomb. Mia was still living with Mianca but they had just found out that Mianca was pregnant so Mia was going to move in with Seantrel today. She was already practically living with him because she spent almost four days out of the week at his house so they might as well have made it official.

"Mia are you sure this is what you want to do," Mianca asked as she helped Mia put the last of her things in a box.

"Yes Mianca, this is something that I should have been done. You're having a baby and you and your husband have never had a chance to go through the newlywed stage. Now you two can Christian the entire house and walk around naked without having to worry about if I'll walk in."

"I'm just saying this might be a little too soon."

"Mianca I love you but you worry too much. Relax and I'll still come to visit you."

"Is this the last of everything," Seantrel asked from the doorway?

"Yeah just these two boxes right here," Mia said.

Mianca grabbed her sister and wrapped her in a tight hug and whispered in her ear "call me no matter what time of day if you need me. I will always be there for you."

Mia hugged Mianca back just as tight and shook her head up and down as a single tear rolled down her face. You would have thought that Mia was moving out of town and not just an hour away.

Seantrel shook his head to himself as he walked out the room thinking *girls.*

Mia went downstairs and gave Isaiah a hug and kiss on the cheek before walking out of the house behind Seantrel.

The drive to Seantrel's house was pretty quiet. Seantrel knew Mia was a little sad about leaving her sister but they both knew it was the right thing to do especially if they wanted their relationship to work. Seantrel found Mianca trying to dictate a few things about it and Seantrel wasn't having that. He felt that if anyone was going to tell Mia what she should or shouldn't do was him. Besides Seantrel felt like his business was just that his. He didn't care who Mianca was, he was in a relationship with Mia, not her.

Seantrel gave Mia the house keys so that she could let herself in the house while he got her things out of his truck. Since Seantrel's house was already fully furnished all Mia had to bring were her clothes and personal items.

Mia opened the door and flopped down on the couch and took her shoes off. She knew that she had just made a huge decision and just hoped that it was the right one. The last thing she wanted to do was go crawling right back home to Mianca.

Seantrel brought the last of Mia's boxes into the house and laid them in the corner of the room. He then pulled her up from the couch and embraced her in a tight bear hug. Seantrel took a long sniff of Mia's hair and exhaled.

"You know I love the scent of this strawberry shampoo you use."

"Thanks baby, it's my favorite too."

"So what do you want for dinner tonight," Seantrel asked?

"I thought I was your dinner tonight," Mia responded.

"Nah my love, you're my snack and dessert," Seantrel said between soft kisses on her neck. "Your man needs real food to keep him strong so I can keep picking you up just the way you like."

"Is that so," Mia said flirtatiously as she stuck her hand down Seantrel's basketball shorts removing his semi-erect penis.

Mia and Seantrel lips found each other as Mia continued to massage his manhood.

Mia broke the kiss and dropped down to her knees in front of Seantrel. She licked her lips before licking up and down Seantrel's shaft like you would do an ice-cream cone. She put the tip in her mouth and sucked as she allowed his dick to go in further.

Seantrel loved the way his dick looked going in and out of Mia's small mouth. He watched as her saliva glistened on it. He grabbed a handful of her hair and massaged her head as she deep throated it. He tried his best not to bust yet but he couldn't help it because the more he moaned and grabbed Mia's head the stronger her jaws locked around his dick and the way she massaged his balls as she sucked turned him on even more.

"Damn girl, you about to make me cum," Seantrel grunted.

Mia paused for a second so that she could say "well cum in my mouth then daddy."

Seantrel's dick instantly jerked as Mia said those words and he released his load down her throat.

Mia removed her mouth and played with the nut that was at the tip of his dick with her finger to give Seantrel a chance to catch his breath.

Once Seantrel's breathing was back to normal Mia stood up and removed her pants before kneeling to suck Seantrel back to life. She played with her clit this time while she sucked him turning herself on even more.

Seantrel's dick was hard enough so he pulled out of Mia's mouth and pushed her back up against the wall. He lifted her up and she wrapped her legs around his waist as his hard penis entered her moist wet spot. They both moaned in ecstasy as Seantrel hit her spot.

"Kiss me like you love me," Seantrel whispered.

Mia removed her arms from around Seantrel's back and placed them around his neck as she gave him one of the most sensual and deep kisses ever. Mia kissed him as if she was trying to suck his soul out of him and make it a part of hers.

Seantrel and Mia made love up against the wall until Mia got her nut off. After Mia came he guided her towards the couch with his dick still inside of her and sat down.

"Ride this dick for me baby, make me cum," Seantrel said before sticking his tongue into Mia's ear.

Mia sat there and rode Seantrel's dick nice and slow until she felt herself squirting on his dick then she picked up the pace so that he could get his now. She closed her eyes as Seantrel lifted her up and down by her hips.

"Open your eyes mama; I want you to watch us cum together."

Mia opened her eyes like Seantrel asked. He loved the lustful and sultry look that was in her eyes whenever they made love.

"You are so damn sexy," Seantrel said right before cumming. Mia rode for a few more seconds before she came right behind him.

"I love you."

"I love you too."

Mia stood up to take the condom off of Seantrel and that's when she realized he didn't have a condom on.

"Seantrel why didn't you put on a condom," Mia whined.

"Relax baby, you're good. I don't have any diseases."
"That's not the point, I still have a semester left of school to go before I graduate. I'm not trying to have a baby."

"Girl you know we would make some gorgeous babies together."

"Whatever," Mia said playfully mushing Seantrel's head before walking upstairs to take a shower.

Mia showered, rubbed on her lotion and then found a pair of boy shorts to put on before going back downstairs.

Seantrel was still sitting on the couch in the same spot in only his boxers.

"I can get use to this," Mia said before sitting down next to him.

"You have no choice, now do you," Seantrel said playfully but seriously.

Mia and Seantrel relaxed on the couch until Seantrel received a call from his mother. He hopped in the shower and then told Mia he'd be back shortly with dinner as well.

Mia used that as time to unpack her things and get everything situated around the house. She wasn't going to be able to get a wink of sleep with all of the clutter that surrounded the living room.

CHAPTER 8

Seantrel drove to his mother's house with his music on low lost in his thoughts. He didn't know what his brother had gotten himself into this time but he was tired of him acting out. Steven was one of those people that acted like the world owed him something. He didn't want to go to school or work. All he wanted to do was hang out in the streets with his friends and half hustle nickel and dime bags.

Seantrel pulled up to his parent's house and parked the car. He hated that his mother and father wouldn't allow him to help move them up out of the hood. They only lived about 20 minutes away from him but it was horrible where they lived at. People stayed outside on the block all day and night. Some people even sat on the stoop like they paid the mortgage there. There was no convincing Mr. and Mrs. Anderson otherwise because that was the first house that they purchased and the same house where they conceived and raised all their children.

Seantrel got out of the car and turned on his alarm before walking up the three stairs to his parent's home.

Seantrel knocked on the door and waited for an answer. He was just about to knock again when his ten year old nephew answered the door.

"What's up unc," Marcus said to Seantrel.

"What's going on knuckle head," Seantrel replied while going in the house.

"Nothing much, trying to get like you."

Where's your mother?"

"She's upstairs in her room with Ashley getting dressed," Marcus said before running up the stairs.

Seantrel walked through the living room and found his mother and father sitting at the kitchen table. He walked over and kissed his mother on the cheek and gave her a hug then walked over to his father and did the same thing before taking a seat.

"So what's going on? You two look super tired."

"We are, between your brother and sister and her kids we gone be in an early grave."

Seantrel rubbed his hands across his head to calm down. "What did they do now mama?"

"Steven still doing the same things he been doing and running with the same crowd. Yesterday he had the police chase him all the way here and they were trying to get in so that they could search this house then your sister act like we the one that laid down and made those three kids that she got running around here. She always going out the door and don't come back in until the middle of the night. We're at the point now where we just want to give them this house and go live somewhere else."

Seantrel shook his head after listening to his mother speak. He loved his siblings to death but there was no way in hell he was going to allow them get away with disrespecting his parent's home. It was bad enough that Steven wasn't doing anything then for Stephanie to be 27 and not do shit and then want to keep on making babies. He was about to put his foot down tonight.

"Mama I been telling you to let me move you two out of here but I know that's not what you really want so let me go talk to them."

Seantrel walked up the stairs to his sister's room and knocked on the door. He could hear scrambling behind the door before it was finally opened. He walked in and closed the door behind him. Steven and Ashley were sitting on the bed and Stephanie was sitting in a chair. Seantrel looked at them all and could see the glossy look in their eyes and he could also smell the scent of weed in the air that was trying to be covered up by air freshener.

"I know the hell y'all ain't in here smoking that shit. Y'all must really be losing your minds."

"I know you ain't come over here thinking you can run shit Mr. I think I'm better than everybody," said Steven.

"Ashley get out, I need to talk to my brother and sister."

Ashley sat there as if Seantrel wasn't talking to her.

"You can't just come in here trying to kick my company out," yelled Stephanie.

Seantrel looked at Stephanie like she had grown another head. "I can't kick your company out? You don't pay one motherfucking bill in this bitch so you shouldn't even be attempting to have company. Now I repeat, Ashley, get the fuck out."

Ashley stood up and grabbed her purse before storming towards the door. "I'll be on the porch; I don't have time to deal with a nigga that's on his period."

Seantrel grabbed Ashley by her arm. "Watch your mouth and don't refer to me as a nigga again. If I didn't call you a bitch then the only thing that you should be calling me is Sean or Seantrel."

Ashley snatched her arm away and walked out of the door slamming it behind her.

Seantrel focused his attention back to his siblings before speaking. "I don't know what the fuck is going on with you two and quite frankly I don't give a fuck. But you need to get your shit together like yesterday. There is no way in hell mama and dad should be stressed over two grown ass kids and their kids.

"Well in my defense," Stephanie said speaking up. "I been asked you could me and the kids come move in with you and you told me no."

Seantrel couldn't believe that Stephanie had just went there with him.

"You know damn well why I told you no. Your kids are reckless, you reckless, and I wasn't about to let you bring all them hood rats and dope boys to my house. I worked to damn hard to get where I am to allow anybody to fuck that up."

"Look y'all two can talk in private. I don't have to sit here and listen to this shit," said Steven as he stood up from the bed.

Seantrel reverted his attention away from Stephanie and focused it on Steven.

"Say what now? You don't have time for this shit?"

"You heard damn well what I said."

"Man you must've forgot who the oldest is. Don't you dare stand here and talk reckless to me like you lost your mind or like I'm one of these niggas on the street and you don't have nothing but time because the last time I checked you didn't have a job."

Steven waved his hand at Seantrel and pushed pass him. Seantrel took that as a sign of disrespect and Steven basically was saying fuck him and what he had to say.

Stephanie saw the look in Seantrel's eyes and knew that things were about to get bad. Stephanie opened her mouth to say something but before she could form the words Seantrel had pinned Steven up against the wall.

"I don't know what the fuck you got going on and I really don't give a fuck but you better get it together. You already know I don't play with you like that. I will fuck you up and then go sit with you in the hospital," Seantrel said through gritted teeth.

"Get your damn hands off of me now," said Steven with just as much venom in his voice.

Seantrel released his grip off of Steven and as soon as he stepped back Steven punched him in the jaw. Seantrel grabbed his jaw for a split second then punched Steven right back.

Stephanie hurriedly opened her bedroom door and yelled down the hall "mama, daddy, come here, hurry up."

Seantrel and Steven was tussling and bustling on Stephanie's bed. Mr. Anderson immediately ran into the bedroom and pulled his two sons apart.

"You two break this shit up now. Y'all to damn old for this; don't kill each other in my house. Take y'all asses outside with it."

Seantrel stormed out of the room but stopped in the door way looking back and forth between Stephanie and Steven. "I know both of you heard what I told you. You have two weeks to get it together or find somewhere else to live."

Seantrel walked out of the house and saw Ashley and was about to storm pass her but she grabbed him by the arm, "wait a minute Seantrel."

Seantrel looked down at his arm and snatched away from her.

"Don't touch me, what do you want?"

"Why do you always have to play me like that? I thought we had something special."

"Ashley, how could you think that? We ain't had sex in almost 5 months and I don't even respond to your text messages or answer your calls."

"That's my point; you treat me like I'm a jump off or something."

Seantrel closed his eyes and twirled his neck around to relax his body.

"Ashley I don't have time for this. You couldn't have possibly thought we were together. We only fucked and got drunk together. The most I ever did was get your hair done a few times or bought you food. We never went out on one date or in public alone."

"Alright well fine, when can I get some dick then?"

"I ain't on that with you Ashley; I got in house pussy right now and a sexy woman to go home to every night. Besides you don't know how to keep your mouth closed."

"I promise I won't say nothing Seantrel," Ashley said half begging.

"We'll see but I have to go because I need to pick up something to eat and get home. I've already been gone long enough," Seantrel said turning around and walking away as Stephanie walked onto the porch.

Stephanie and Ashley watched as Seantrel pulled off before either of them decided to speak.

"Why didn't you tell me that Seantrel had a new girlfriend?'

"You know I don't get involved in my brother's business but she seems like a cool chick to me."

"Wait a minute, you've been around her? I thought I was your best friend Steph."

"So what, that's my brother and you know he doesn't play that."

Ashley was really upset that Stephanie never told her about Seantrel's girlfriend and the fact that she had been around her a few times.

"So is that your new best friend now?"

"What? Who are you talking about?"

"Seantrel's new bitch," Ashley said folding her arms.

"Are you fucking serious right now? You sound real crazy with your line of questioning. Let me find out my little brother got your nose wide open," Stephanie said jokingly.

Ashley laughed it off not wanting Stephanie to know that she was speaking the truth.

"So are we going to get out of here or what?" Ashley asked changing the subject.

"Yeah, just let me run in and get my purse and change my shoes."

"Alright," Ashley said before refocusing her attention to the guys hanging out on the block.

Ashley stood there in deep thought trying to figure out what she could do in order to get Seantrel to pay attention to her again. He was going to be her meal ticket out of the hood. She was happy when Seantrel moved out of his parent's house and purchased his own home. It showed the type of man he was and that's what separated him from the rest.

Ashley pulled out her cell phone and wrote Seantrel a text message.

I'm sorry for the way I acted tonight. I know I shouldn't have let my attitude get in the way. I'll be here waiting when you ready. I love you baby! Xoxoxo

"You ready to go," asked Stephanie startling Ashley.

"Yeah let's go."

Ashley and Stephanie hopped in Ashley's brother car and headed to the club for the night.

CHAPTER 9

Seantrel pulled up to his house and looked down at his phone and saw that he had a missed call and text from Ashley. He read the text that was from Ashley and shook his head before pressing delete without even bothering about responding to it.

Seantrel walked into the house and laid the food on the table before going in the kitchen to get some plates and something to drink. He walked up the stairs to see where Mia was and found her laid across the bed with a book in her hands. He slid the book out of her hands and shook her lightly.

"Baby wake up."

Mia stirred in bed then turned around and smiled before opening her eyes. Once she opened her eyes her smile turned into a frown.

"What happened to you baby?" Mia asked as she set up.

Seantrel's tank top was ripped and he had a welt on his neck.

"I'll tell you while we eat, now come on and get up. I'm sorry it took so long."

Mia climbed out of bed and headed down the stairs towards the living room couch. She had unpacked most of her boxes and only had a few more to go but she set those in the closet and would finish unpacking them at a later date.

Mia and Seantrel sat and ate while Seantrel talked about everything that went on at his mother's house minus the bullshit with Ashley. Mia hated that Seantrel was stressed and there wasn't anything that she could do about it. It felt as if she could feel the same pain that Seantrel was feeling. She was at the point now where she was realizing that she never loved Dante the way she thought she did.

"Baby I have a question. Do you think we're moving too fast," asked Mia?

"Do you love me," Seantrel asked seriously?

"Of course I do, you already know that."

"Then that's all that matters, it's just me and you now."

Mia looked into Seantrel's eyes and saw his sincerity and smiled before she kissed him softly on the lips.

Mia and Seantrel finished eating before she went into the kitchen to wash the dishes while Seantrel went upstairs to take a shower in the master's bathroom.

Seantrel laid his phone on the top of the toilet before getting in the shower. He lathered the soap on his body then started singing. He didn't realize that Mia had walked into their bedroom. She sat on the bed and recorded Seantrel singing while busting up laughing. He sounded like a cat getting run over and it didn't make it any better that he was singing "Nothing in this world" by Keke Wyatt and Avant.

Seantrel climbed out of the shower and dried off before walking into the room.

Mia pressed play on the phone letting Seantrel hear the recording of him. He ran over to her and tried to snatch the phone but she held her arms behind her back. He reached out and started tickling her before she had no choice but to let it go so that she could grab his hands.

"Ok, ok, ok, I quit." Mia laughed.

Seantrel sat Mia up then went back to the recording so that he could delete it.

"Nooooo, don't delete it, it's cute baby, I promise I won't share it with anyone," Mia said looking at Seantrel with puppy dog eyes.

Seantrel couldn't resist that look that Mia gave him. She always got what she wanted when she did it and she knew it worked like a charm.

"Fine," Seantrel said passing her the phone back.

Seantrel stood back up and went into the bathroom to get his phone when he saw that he had a missed call and voicemail. He held down the number one key in order to listen to his voicemail.

Damn you could've at least replied to my text message and said something back. Why the fuck is you tripping so hard? I know that bitch ain't got it like that and I know some young ass broad can't do you like I can. You better wake up before you lose your chance.

Seantrel replayed the message again and his blood bubbled. He was tempted to call Ashley's ass back but he had something better for her. He sent Stephanie a text to find out where they were before he went back into the bedroom.

"Are you too tired to go out with your man? Stephanie left me a voicemail saying she wanted me to meet up with her and I don't want to leave you at home alone on your first night here," Seantrel said half lying.

He lied about Stephanie calling but the part about not wanting to leave her at home alone was the truth. Mia was the type of woman that he wanted to have outside with him so that he could show her off to the world. She was officially his trophy girl.

"I'm never too tired to go out with you my love. Just let me find something to put on."

Mia went in the closet and pulled out an all white jumpsuit and a red pair of Christian Louboutin heels with a matching red handbag and her red leather jacket.

Seantrel watched as she applied her eye shadow, mascara, and a light coat of gloss before slipping into her jumpsuit and heels.

"How do I look?" Mia asked as she spun around.

"You look so good that I need to get up and throw my clothes on before we don't make it out of this house."

Mia's jumpsuit clung to her body like it was custom made just for her. Mia stood there looking like an hourglass to Seantrel. She had perky 36dd breast, a flat stomach, thin waist, thick thighs and an even thicker ass. She wore her 165 pounds well.

Seantrel put on a pair of black jeans, a red button up shirt, a pair of black Steve Madden shoes, and a black Pelle jacket.

By the time Seantrel and Mia made it to the car Stephanie had replied to Seantrel's message and sent the name of the club they were at.

Seantrel drove to club "Adrianna's" which was only about 10 minutes away from his house since there wasn't any traffic outside.

Seantrel couldn't find any decent parking space so he hahis car valet parked before getting out. He walked around and helped Mia out of the car. They both walked right up to the front of the line and Seantrel said a few words to the bouncer before they gave each other some dap and he let them through.

"I see you know everybody," Mia said to Seantrel.

"Yeah I use to come here all the time so a lot of them still remember me."

Seantrel talked to one of the hostess and bought a bottle of Coconut Ciroc so that they could go sit in the V.I.P area. As soon as they made it up the stairs Seantrel recognized a few guys from his old neighborhood and spotted Stephanie. She wasn't paying any attention though so he sat in the section that was reserved for him and sent Stephanie a text with his location.

By the time Stephanie made it over to Seantrel the waitress had brought over their liquor and glasses already.

"Hey Mia, how are you doing?"

"Hey Stephanie, I'm good, how about you?"

"Not as good as you," Stephanie replied referring to the way Mia was dressed.

A few of the guys and some chicks that were with them came over to Seantrel's area with their own bottles and sat down. Everyone was laughing and having a good time until Ashley and Steven came over to where everyone was at.

"So this where you disappeared to bitch," Ashley said to Stephanie.

"Yeah, I came over here to chill with Seantrel for a minute."

Ashley hadn't realized that Seantrel was sitting there at first. She walked over to where he was stumbling slightly like she had too much to drink.

"My feet hurt and it looks like there's no more seats so I guess I can sit here," Ashley said as she sat on Seantrel's lap and bumped into Mia making her spill some of her drink.

Stephanie stood there in shock with her mouth wide open not believing what Ashley was doing.

"Excuse you," Mia said standing up from her seat looking down at Ashley and Seantrel.

"Ashley, get the fuck up off of me before I knock your ass on this floor," Seantrel said through gritted teeth as he pushed her up off of him.

Ashley stood face to face with Mia.

"So, this young bitch the one that got you tripping," asked Ashley?

Seantrel jumped up from his seat after Ashley spoke those words but Steven ran over and grabbed him.

"Don't do it bro, she ain't worth it."

Steven and Seantrel always had they differences but they always made sure to have each other's back as well. There was no way he was going to allow Seantrel to go to jail for beating Ashley's ass.

Mia turned her head and looked at Seantrel then back at Ashley before speaking.

"I don't know what the fuck you two had going on but that shit is over with. I mean completely motherfucking dead. Don't you ever disrespect me and act like I'm not here.

You better get your feelings and stick them in those raggedy ass jean pockets. You ain't anywhere near my level to even try and step on my toes. Oh and don't ever address me as anything except Mia you cheap hoe."

Ashley stood there stuck on stupid and stunned that Mia had actually talked to her that way in front of an entire crowd.

Stephanie stood there embarrassed and embarrassed for her friend because she had never seen anyone step up to Ashley like that. Everyone always allowed Ashley to get away with her bullshit or just brushed it off afraid of what she might do or say but when the shoe was on the other foot she was completely quiet.

Mia waited there for a minute to see was Ashley going to get out of her body but after she got no response she refocused her attention back to Seantrel and smiled.

"Come on baby let's get out of here, it's a bit too crowded now."

Seantrel just walked over and grabbed Mia's hand without saying anything.

Mia stopped and looked at Stephanie, "it was nice seeing you again, and we need to do lunch one day."

Stephanie's mouth said "alright" but her mind was saying "this is one crazy bitch."

Stephanie watched Seantrel and Mia walk down the stairs before walking over to Ashley.

Stephanie opened her mouth to say something but Ashley stormed right pass her and down the stairs.

Everyone in the area started to snicker and laugh at Ashley.

Stephanie looked at them then rushed down the stairs to try and catch up with her friend.

"Ashley, hold up," Stephanie yelled as she caught up with her.

Ashley waited until she got outside and then stopped walking allowing Stephanie to catch up. She looked from side to side to see if she saw Seantrel or Mia. When she didn't see either one of them she started walking again towards her car.

Stephanie had to practically run to keep up with Ashley. As soon as they made it to the car Ashley snapped.

"What the fuck was that back there? You are supposed to be my best friend and you let that bitch embarrass me. She lucky we were in the club or I would've fucked her up."

"What do you mean I let her embarrass you? No ma'am that was all you on your own. You're my best friend and I love you but you were dead ass wrong. You knew that was his girlfriend and you decided to play yourself and disrespect her in the process."

"So you taking that bitch side again?"

Stephanie took a deep breath and shook her head at Ashley. She couldn't believe that she was actually trying to play victim.

"Ashley you are too old for this shit. If you want to look at it as me taking her side then so be it. You know if it was the other way around you would've been in there ready to fight."

Ashley sat there and listened to Stephanie talk. She knew it was truth in Stephanie's words but she wasn't willing to admit it right now.

"So how old is that girl anyway? Is your brother robbing the cradle?" Ashley asked not bothering to comment on anything else that was said.

"I think he said she's 21 or 22."

"Well he better leave that baby at home next time because I'm not going to be so nice."

Stephanie rolled her eyes and remained quiet. She was tired of wasting her breath and time with Ashley. All she wanted to do was get far away from Ashley and go in the house and relax so that she could reevaluate her life.

A lot of the things that Seantrel said to her and Steven made a lot of sense and she was going to go home and make sure she had a talk with Steven too before it was too late for him. If Seantrel could get his life together and move on then nothing was stopping them from doing the same thing as well.

"So you're just going to sit here quiet for the remainder of the night," asked Ashley?

"No, you can actually take me home; I need to get up early in the morning."

Ashley looked over at Stephanie before focusing her attention back on the road. Ashley knew that she had fucked up and it was best if she remained quiet and gave Stephanie a chance to cool off.

Ashley pulled up to Stephanie's house and Stephanie got out of the car without even saying a word. Her mind was all over the place as she walked in the house. She dialed

Seantrel's number to check on him but he didn't answer the phone. She hoped everything was cool with him and this situation didn't cause him too many problems at home.

Stephanie took a shower and then checked her phone to see did Seantrel call back. Just as she expected it wasn't a missed call from him so that meant he was probably upset with her as well. She didn't bother calling him back she just ended up sending a text instead then got ready for bed.

CHAPTER 10

Seantrel looked down at his phone and saw Stephanie calling and hit ignore before hanging up the phone. He partially blamed himself for what had taken place. He wanted to make Ashley jealous but he didn't think things would go as far as it did. Never did he think that Ashley would push up on him the way that she did in front of Mia. Mia seemed like she was taking the situation better then he was. He expected her to yell and fuss at him but the only thing she said to him when they got in the house was that he needed to learn how to control his hoes better and then she went upstairs to go to sleep.

Seantrel tried his best to fall asleep but his mind was racing too much for him to fall right off to sleep. He looked over and saw Mia was sound asleep. He didn't want to wake her so he grabbed his phone and went downstairs to call Ashley. He didn't care if she was sleep or not. If he couldn't sleep that meant she wasn't allowed to sleep either.

"Hello!" Ashley answered on the first ring.

"I don't know what the fuck is going on with you or what was going through your head when you pulled that stunt but you better not let that shit happen again. If you see me with my girl don't even look my fucking way."

"I'm sorry Seantrel, I had a little too much to drink and I know I was way out of hand but I was in my feelings from the way you were treating me."

"You were sending me messages like you were a fucking crazy person. Since when did we start texting the words I love you?"

"That's the thing Seantrel; I have always loved you but just never said anything."

"I'm sorry that you fell in love with me, it was never my intentions to allow your feelings to get involved but I don't love you. I'm in love with Mia, I got to go," Seantrel said before hanging up and throwing his phone on the couch.

Seantrel went in the kitchen and grabbed a beer before going back up to his bedroom. He laid down in the bed and turned the TV on low and opened his beer.

"I hope you was down there deading that shit," Mia said without turning around.

Seantrel grabbed her and turned her around where her head could lay on his chest.

"You don't have to worry about me and her baby. It's been over between us as soon as I started dating you" he said lying. Seantrel hadn't completely stopped sleeping with Ashley off top. He waited a month and then broke things off with her in his own mind.

"Then why is she tripping?"

"You already know how chicks start to act when they can't have what they want. But it's all about you lil mama," Seantrel said before kissing Mia on the top of her head.

Mia smiled then closed her eyes and fell right back to sleep.

Seantrel finished his beer and watching "Don't be a Menace" before he finally fell asleep as well.

The next morning Seantrel woke up around 12:30 and could smell food coming from the kitchen. He went and used the bathroom and brushed his teeth before going down to the kitchen to see what smelt so good. Mia was standing at the counter with one of his tank tops on and nothing else on up under it chopping up some fruit. The sight of her round ass instantly made his dick hard.

Seantrel walked over to Mia and wrapped his arms around her waist.

"What is that you got on that smells so good?"

"That would be the cake in the oven that I'm baking for desert."

"So what's for dinner?"

"I'm cooking smothered pork chops, rice, and fresh green beans."

"Damn that sound like it's going to be good," Seantrel said as he placed soft kisses on Mia's neck and rubbed his hands in between her thighs making her instantly moist. He bent her over the counter and pulled his dick out of his boxers and entered her. He fucked Mia nice and hard at the kitchen counter until her body was convulsing and she was begging him to make her cum. He wanted to fuck her a little longer but he didn't want her cake to burn up. So as soon as she busted her nut he came right behind her.

Mia took her cake out of the oven then followed Seantrel up to the bathroom so that they could finish where they left off at.

Seantrel and Mia spent that Sunday sucking, fucking, licking, and enjoying each other's company.

The next morning Mia woke up before Seantrel and kissed him on the forehead before heading out to work.

Mia drove to work on cloud nine. She loved spending the entire day locked in the house with Seantrel. They shared a lot with each other about their lives and she had finally told Seantrel how her brother had passed away. She still wanted to pinch herself to make sure she wasn't dreaming because she never thought her life could change so much in so little time.

Mia pulled up to her job and parked. As soon as she got out of the car LaShon was pulling up.

"Hey look at you lady, glowing and shit," LaShon said seriously as she hugged her best friend.

"Hey baby girl, he been doing what it do," Mia said with a laugh.

"Well I'm just glad that you're happy mama, you really deserve it."

"Thank you; now hush before you make me cry."

LaShon laughed at Mia before following her into the building.

Mia's day had been going great so far until 4:00 when it was time to go home. As soon as she walked out of the office she received a call from Dante. He hadn't called her in months so she couldn't understand why he was calling now. She still hadn't told Seantrel about him but she never seemed to find the perfect time to do so.

As soon as her phone stopped ringing she called the correctional billing service and cancelled her account so that she couldn't receive any more phone calls from him or the prison.

Mia called Mianca and talked to her during the drive home. She loved her job but she was going to have to transfer soon or find something else closer because she didn't want to have to continue to do that 45 minute drive every day.

Mia made it to the house and Seantrel was still at work. He didn't get off work until 6:00 so he usually wouldn't make it home until almost 7:00.

Mia started dinner and finished some homework until she heard Seantrel come in. They ended up having a nice relaxing evening watching movies until they fell asleep.

CHAPTER 11

The next couple of months went by smoothly for Mia. She didn't have any more run-ins from Ashley and she found a new job closer to her house doing the same thing but getting paid more. She was missing her family and couldn't wait to see her father on Friday. He was coming from Kentucky to visit her and Mianca for the weekend.

Mia was sitting on the couch eating a bowl of cereal when she got a funny feeling in the pit of her stomach. She placed the bowl on the table and ran into the guest bathroom and threw up all the contents of her stomach. She continued to heave even when nothing else was coming out.

Mia went upstairs to the master's bathroom and brushed her teeth before going back down stairs to dump the bowl of cereal into the toilet. She felt sluggish and no longer had an appetite. She picked up her phone as she lay down on the couch and dialed LaShon's phone number.

"Hello," LaShon answered after the third ring.

"Hey, what you got going on?"

"Nothing really, I'm just sitting here chilling before class. What about you?"

"Sitting here sick but you know I got to get ready to get out of here today too so I can take these finals."

"Can you believe it, once you ace all these finals you will be finished with school."

"Yes, those long summer classes paid off."

Mia and LaShon talked on the phone for a little while longer until Mia had to get up and ready for class.

Mia pulled up to her school and sent Seantrel a text letting him know that she loved and missed him. He had been on a business trip for the last couple of days and she couldn't wait for him to come home later on that night.

Mia walked into the school and wasn't paying attention to where she was going and walked right into somebody.

"Oh, I'm sorry," Mia apologized.

"It's alright beautiful," said the stranger.

His deep baritone voice made Mia instantly look up. The man standing in front of her was dark skinned, sexy and had a nice muscular build. Mia had to smile at him and hurry up and try to walk away before she got herself in trouble but the sexy man wasn't letting her get away that easy.

"I'm Donavan, what's your name?"

"I'm Mia," she said nervously.

"Well Ms. Mia can I get your number and maybe call you sometime."

"That wouldn't be a good idea, I'm in a relationship."

Donavan gave her his sexy smile before speaking again.

"That's fine; I could always use a new friend. Just take my number down and if you ever decide to use it then that's fine by me."

Mia reluctantly saved Donavan's number in her phone before walking away.

Mia took her seat in class and shook her head so that she could focus on her test. She knew she should have deleted Donavan's phone number as soon as she walked away but something inside her wouldn't allow it.

Mia took her exam and was finished in 45 minutes. She usually would wait around until everyone was finished before getting up and walking out but her stomach was hurting like crazy so she handed the teacher the test and exited the class. She pulled her phone out and read the text from Seantrel.

I love you too baby, my flight just landed so I'll be home shortly.

Mia smiled at the text then sent a text to LaShon.

Sorry babez I got to get home, I'm really not feeling well. Call my phone later on.

Mia left school and went right to Walgreens and bought a home pregnancy test, saltine crackers and a 7-up pop.

As soon as Mia made it in the house she ran right to the bathroom and peed on the stick. She waited anxiously for the results. The three minutes seemed like it was taking forever. Once her timer went off she checked the stick and just as she thought she was pregnant. She wasn't sad or excited about the situation.

Mia and Seantrel made enough money separately and combined to take care of a child. She was finished with school and all she had to do was walk across the stage in July. Her only issue was what Seantrel would think about the situation.

Mia wrapped the test up in toilet paper and went to lie down on the couch with her ginger ale, crackers and thoughts. Once Seantrel made it in she would just tell him the news and take it from there.

CHAPTER 12

Seantrel drove with the music low on his way home from the airport.

"Seantrel why you got to drop me off then leave?"

Seantrel looked over at the female passenger before speaking.

"Jasmine you already know why I got to drop you off and keep it moving."

"So this weekend meant nothing to you?"

"Please don't start it with the wining, you asked me to spend the weekend with you for your birthday and that's what I did. What more do you want from me?"

Jasmine looked at Seantrel and was about to say something smart but changed her mind.

"I want you Seantrel, all of you," Jasmine said on the verge of tears.

"I can't give you all of me; you knew this from the beginning."

"Seantrel we having been fucking for almost three months. You need to just leave that bitch alone and be with me. It's obvious you ain't happy with her or you wouldn't have spent the weekend with me."

Seantrel looked at Jasmine then back at the road without speaking. He knew that he shouldn't have gone on the trip with her to Vegas with her but he was being nice since she didn't have anybody else to go with. It seemed like the moment he started being nice to bitches they started thinking that he had real feelings for them and could take his main bitch place. He went through this every week with someone. He didn't know how many ways to let them know Mia wasn't going anywhere.

"So you're just not going to say anything," Jasmine asked Seantrel.

Seantrel turned his radio up and didn't even bother about looking her way.

"You are such a jerk," yelled Jasmine!

Seantrel looked at her and burst out laughing.

"You know you are sexy when you mad."

Jasmine rolled her eyes at Seantrel, she hated when he changed the subject so fast.

"Oh you still mad at me," asked Seantrel.

When Jasmine didn't respond Seantrel reached his right hand over into Jasmine's lap and lifted her dress up. He played with the brim of her panties before sticking his hands inside of them. He slid his hand down until his fingers found her clit. He rubbed it in a circular motion until he heard her start to moan. He slid his fingers down a little further and stuck one inside of her and then two more.

"I hate you Seantrel," Jasmine moaned out and she closed her eyes opened her legs a little wilder. Seantrel kept his eyes on the road the entire time but he could hear Jasmine's breath speeding up and knew that she was ready to cum so he used his thumb and rubbed her clit faster as he finger fucked her just as fast. He could feel her pussy contracting and felt her cum slide down his hand.

"You still hate me?" Seantrel asked with a smirk.

"You know I don't hate you baby."

"Then show daddy how much you like him," Seantrel said as he unzipped his pants.

Jasmine licked her lips as she removed Seantrel's dick from his pants and slow stroked it. When it was hard she spit on it then took a deep breath and placed his dick in his mouth. Jasmine wasn't like the other chicks that gave him head. She could take half his dick in her mouth without having to play around. She knew the true definition of deep throating. She sucked his dick until she could feel his balls up against her chin then she tightened her jaws to use her mouth as a suction.

Seantrel grabbed a handful of her hair and tried his best to keep his eyes opened so that they didn't crash into anything. About five minutes later Seantrel was cumming.

Jasmine sat up and wiped the side of her mouth before kissing Seantrel on the cheek.

During the duration of the drive to Jasmine's house everything seemed back to normal between Seantrel and Jasmine until he pulled up to her house and stopped in the middle of the street.

"Why are you sitting here in the streets? Aren't you going to park and come in so we can finish what we started?"

"No, I already told you I wasn't coming in, ain't nothing changed about that."

"But I'm horny now and I know you are too."

"I am horny and that's why I'm about to go home."

"Wow so you used me to suck your dick and now you about to go home and fuck her."

Seantrel shook his head at Jasmine, "correction, I'm about to go home and make love to her. You're the one that I fuck."

Jasmine grabbed her bag out of the car and slammed Seantrel's door. Seantrel pulled off without even bothering about making sure she got in the house.

Seantrel drove to Baskin Robbins down the street from his house and grabbed Mia a container of cookies and cream ice cream. It was her favorite so he knew she would love it.

Seantrel pulled up to the house and didn't see Mia's car but he knew she should have been home by now. He parked in the driveway and went in the house and turned on the lights and didn't see Mia. He went and put her ice cream in the freezer and then went upstairs to their bedroom to see if she was up there. He walked into the bedroom and saw candles and the lights dimly lit.

"Mia," Seantrel called out.

Mia walked out of the bathroom with a gold pair of stilettos and a red negligee on.

"Damn you look good," Seantrel said taken back from Mia's beauty.

Seantrel walked over to Mia and lifted her up and gave her a delicate kiss on her lips. Mia wrapped her legs around his waist and kissed him deeper. When Mia felt Seantrel's hand slide up under her negligee she broke the kiss and slid from his arms.

"Not yet daddy, we'll get to that in a little while."

81

Mia undressed Seantrel and led him to the bathtub of water that she ran for him. Seantrel slid into the hot bath water and laid his head against the back of the tub.

"How did you know I was on my way?"

"I didn't, I had already started on your water and when I heard you pull up I added more hot water."

"You're amazing and I love you," said Seantrel.

"I love you too baby and I have something to tell you," Mia said nervously.

Seantrel saw the look on Mia's face and set up straight in the tub.

"What's wrong baby?"

"I'm pregnant," Mia blurted out and held her breath as she waited on Seantrel's response.

"You're going to have my baby, that's great news," Seantrel yelled!

Mia let out her breath and allowed her breathing to get back to normal.

Seantrel pulled Mia in the tub with him and kissed her deeply with one of the most passionate kisses she had ever received. She was glad that he was taking the news well.

Seantrel was excited about having a baby with Mia. He couldn't think of a better person to have his babies. He knew that she loved him for him and not for what he could do for her. Mia would be the perfect wife.

Seantrel undressed Mia as she washed his body. Once she finished washing him he returned the favor. They turned on the shower water and rinsed each other body's off. Seantrel picked Mia up and led her to the bed. He rubbed lotion on her body then laid her down on the bed.

Seantrel spread Mia's thighs and dived in head first. He twirled his tongue around her clit and stuck one of his fingers in her pussy. Mia lifted her legs higher and squeezed them tightly around Seantrel's neck. .Mia's body began to shake as her body climaxed.

Seantrel placed his dick at Mia's opening and gently went in and out of her. A slight moan escaped her lips as Seantrel hit her spot. Seantrel lifted Mia's leg in the crook of his arm and went in and out of her nice slowly.

"Hmmm….. Damn, shit, right there baby," Mia moaned out in ecstasy. Seantrel was sucking and fucking her and she loved every bit of it. She took in his nine inch curve like a pro as he continued to hit the bottom of her vagina canal. The more she moaned out in pleasure the deeper Seantrel went. She felt like she was at the point of no return.

Seantrel took Mia on a rollercoaster ride he took her all the way to the top then brought her to the middle but stopped before she made it to the bottom. He had her ready to pull out her hair from the unexplainable pleasure.

Seantrel had Mia speaking in a different language.

"Ca fait du bien papa," Mia whispered in Seantrel's ear.

Seantrel had the slightest clue of what Mia was saying but it turned him on even more.

"Say something else to me baby," Seantrel moaned.

"Voulez vous coucher avec moi cer soir, voulez vouis coucher avec moi," Mia purred.

Mia wrapped her legs around Seantrel's torso and dug her fingers into his back. She was almost positive that she had left a few scratches. She didn't intend to hurt him but she couldn't help it. The dick was just too good to her. If you took a picture of her feet you'd think she was throwing up gang signs with her toes.

Mia had never had another man make love to her the way Seantrel was doing. Seantrel was teaching Mia how every part of her body worked from the top of her head to the bottom of her toes. He was introducing her to pleasure points that she never even knew existed.

Mia was on the verge of cumming for the fifth time that night and Seantrel had barely broke a sweat. He was like the energizer bunny that kept going and going, the stamina he had was unimaginable and it was all natural. Mia was on cloud nine and ready to float away.

Mia loved how Seantrel always took her to her highest peak and caught her before she made it to the bottom. She was falling madly in love with Seantrel and there wasn't anything that anybody could do about it.

CHAPTER 13

The next morning Mia woke up and went downstairs to cook breakfast. She made pancakes, omelets, diced potatoes, and fresh squeezed orange juice. She placed the food on a tray and took it upstairs to their bedroom.

Seantrel was in the bed snoring so Mia laid the tray on the table and shook him until he finally woke up.

"Come on baby, I'm tired," Seantrel fussed.

"But I made you breakfast so get up."

Seantrel looked at the food Mia cooked and sat up and kissed her.

"Damn, I need to go out of town more often," Seantrel joked.

"Very funny, just eat your food."

"Why don't you call off today so that we can do a walk-in to set up your prenatal," suggested Seantrel.

"I already thought ahead of you and called off already."

Seantrel and Mia ate breakfast and got dressed before heading to the clinic not far from their house.

Mia signed in and filled out the paperwork in the clinic. They were called in to the back within 30 minutes top.

The medical assistant weighed Mia and she looked down at the scale and saw that is said 160 pounds. It was just her luck that she had lost five pounds right when she was about to start gaining weight. They checked all of Mia's vitals before giving her a cup to urinate in. Mia released her bladder then went and met Seantrel in the examination room. They talked for a little while before the doctor came in.

"Hello I'm doctor Mahogany Evans and I'll be your gynecologist."

"Hi, I'm Mia and this is my boyfriend Seantrel."

Doctor Evans asked Mia a few questions as far as when was her last menstrual cycle and what type of diet had she been on. The doctor checked the wheel cycle and calculated that Mia was about six weeks pregnant.

Doctor Evans had Mia to undress completely then performed her examination. She stuck two fingers inside of Mia to make sure that everything was alright with Mia's cervix. Everything seemed fine so she removed her hands and changed her gloves.

"Your examination is almost finished we just have to check your baby's heartbeat. Now this gel might be a little cool so don't be alarmed."

Doctor Evans squirted a little gel on Mia's stomach and she jumped lightly which cause Seantrel to burst into laughter.

"Ain't nothing funny punk," Mia hissed.

Doctor Evans rubbed the fetal monitor over Mia's lower abdomen and it didn't take long for her to find the fetus. The baby had a strong heart beat and the sound instantly warmed Mia and Seantrel's heart. They both had a Europhobic feeling and were happy to be able to share this opportunity with each other.

Seantrel leaned over and kissed Mia on the lips.

"We're going to make great parents to our child," Seantrel said seriously and meant every word of it.

Mia got dressed and Doctor Evans gave her an appointment for next month and faxed over her prescription for prenatal and iron pills to Walgreen's.

Mia and Seantrel left the clinic hand in hand. They both agreed not to tell anyone about the pregnancy until her birthday because they wouldn't have no way of hiding the reason she wasn't drinking.

Seantrel and Mia went to Walgreen's and grabbed her prescriptions and some anti-nauseous medication because Mia's stomach felt like it was doing summersaults. She didn't know how long she would be able to deal with the sickness and it was only the beginning of the pregnancy. She prayed that it wouldn't last long.

Seantrel led Mia in the house and took her upstairs to the bedroom. He helped her undress as she lay down in bed.

"Baby I'm going to make you some soup then I'll be back up."

"I'm not hungry Seantrel, my stomach hurts."

"You have to eat something you can't be starving my baby. You haven't eaten anything since breakfast and you threw half of that shit up so just lay here and relax."

Mia knew it was no reasoning with Seantrel so she just closed her eyes and turned over on her side.

Seantrel went downstairs in the kitchen and pulled out a can of chicken noodle progressive soup out of the cabinet with a bowl and pot. He poured the soup in the can and turned the stove on medium.

Seantrel went to get a spoon out of the drawer when his phone started vibrating. He looked down at the phone and answered it angrily.

"What the fuck are you doing calling me?"

"I missed you baby, I'm not allowed to call you now," asked Jasmine?

"I know you got the text that I sent you this morning saying Mia was not going to work."

Seantrel could hear Jasmine blow air out her mouth before speaking.

"So I guess that means I'll just talk to you when you get to work then."

"No you won't, I'm not going to work today so please don't call my phone back today or tonight," Seantrel said before hanging the phone up on Jasmine.

Seantrel stirred up Mia's soup and poured it in a bowl. He made sure to put his phone on silent before he went upstairs to the room just in case Jasmine wanted to be on some bullshit and callback.

As soon as Seantrel got up to the room he took his phone out of his pocket and plugged it into its charger. He could see the led light blinking which meant he had a new message but he ignored it and began to feed Mia her soup.

Once Mia ate half of her soup and drunk some of the 7-Up she felt a little better. She took her prenatal pill and then dosed off to sleep while Seantrel played NBA Live on his XBOX. Once he saw that Mia was all the way sleep he picked up his phone and unlocked it. He had three missed calls and two text messages from Jasmine.

Seantrel read the first message out loud.

I know that you can see me calling you. You need to gone somewhere with bullshit.

Seantrel hit delete then read the next text message.

Your ass just ain't gone be satisfied until I start hating you for real.

Seantrel deleted that message as well then added Jasmine to his block list. He had a trick for her. If she wanted to play then he was going to play too.

The next morning Seantrel called his job and had them switch his entire schedule around so that he would never run into Jasmine at work. Plus it would give him more time to help Mia out until she was feeling better.

Seantrel felt that if a bitch couldn't play by his rules then he would just cut them off completely. Ashley had learned the hard way now Jasmine's turn to do the same.

CHAPTER 14

The past two weeks had gone by pretty good for Mia. She was finally able to hold her food down and she wasn't feeling nauseated all the time. It was perfect timing since today was Seantrel's birthday dinner and she couldn't wait to celebrate with her man. They rented out a hall for him and it was an all black grown and sexy affair.

"Baby hurry up or we're going to be late," Seantrel yelled up the stairs to Mia.

"Give me one minute," Mia yelled as she finished the finishing touches of her makeup.

Mia grabbed her purse off the bed and headed down the stairs to meet Seantrel.

"Damn ma, you look breath taking but should you be wearing those shoes?" Seantrel asked referring to her 4 ½ silver sling back pumps.

"They're fine baby; I have extra shoes to take with me just in case."

Mia and Seantrel walked out to Seantrel's car looking and feeling like a million bucks.

Seantrel looked like he belonged on the cover of GQ with his custom made 3 piece silver and black Versace suit with silver Rolex and a pair of Silver Stacy Adams.

Mia was dressed in a black custom fitted long Versace dress that went to her ankles with a split all the way up to her upper thigh with the back cut out and a v-neck slit down to her breast. She had a silver purse to match with a diamond jewelry set that contained a chain, earrings, and bracelet which was all an early birthday present for her from Seantrel.

Seantrel and Mia walked into the hall and Seantrel was impressed with how good everything looked. He allowed Mia and Stephanie to take care of everything as far as decorations, food and the DJ. The décor looked great to Seantrel. There was huge happy birthday banner with black and silver table cloths with streamers and centerpieces.

"This looks good ma," Seantrel said as kissed Mia on the cheek.

"Thanks my love!"

Seantrel walked around and greeted some of his guest before it was time to sit down and eat. He noticed Ashley and Jasmine were there and gave them both a look that said "don't start no shit.:" He could understand why Ashley was there she was a friend of the family and Stephanie's best friend but he knew Jasmine being there was some bullshit. She must've seen the invitations at the job or came with one of his co-workers. Either way it was all good as long as she didn't show her ass because he was through with her anyway.

Stephanie came and led Mia over to a table. The table was set up for Mia, Seantrel, and his parents, Stephanie, Steven, Mianca and Isaiah.

Mia and Seantrel walked over and greeted everyone that was seated at the table before they took their seats. Mianca was sitting on the other side of Mia and Mrs. Anderson was sitting on the other side of Seantrel. Mia rubbed Mianca's protruding stomach. She was showing now and Mia couldn't wait until her niece or nephew was brought into the world.

The caterers brought the food out and laid it on each table. The food was buffet style and it was more than enough for everyone. They had fried chicken, baked chicken, tilapia, mashed potatoes, green beans, and rolls.

Mia looked down at her plate and prayed that she didn't get sick and ended up throwing up everywhere.

Everyone was in the middle of eating, laughing and talking when Seantrel stood up and said that he wanted to propose a toast. Everyone lifted their glasses as Seantrel said a speech.

"I would like to thank everyone that has come out to spend my 27th birthday with me. I was actually surprised at the turn out being what the dress code was but you all came to show out for your boy and you look good doing it. I have to give special thanks to my sister Stephanie," Seantrel said as he looked over to her. "Stephanie you and I have our differences all the time but you didn't hesitate when I asked you to help me out for my party and I love you for that."

"I love you too, now hurry up before you make me cry," Stephanie said smiling.

There were a lot of awww's throughout before Seantrel turned his attention to Mia.

"Mia words can't explain how much my life has changed since you entered my life. I love everything about you from your smile, style, and even the way you say my name. I am grateful for meeting you in that club that night. I just have one question for you," Seantrel said as he turned Mia's chair around to face him.

Mia heard those words and instantly started screaming on the inside from excitement. She knew that they could only mean one thing.

Seantrel reached into his pocket and took out a jewelry box and got down on one knee and opened it.

"Will you marry me Mia?"

Mia slowly looked down at the most beautiful 3karat princess diamond cut ring she had ever seen and her eyes begin to glisten.

"Yes, I'll marry you baby."

Seantrel stood up and lifted Mia out of her chair and kissed her gently on the lips. The room erupted with applause.

Jasmine wasn't too happy about it though because she stood up and stormed out of the room. Seantrel caught it because he looking right at her when he got down on his knee.

"Baby this ring is beautiful," Mia said in awe.

"Not as beautiful as you," Seantrel said immediately making Mia blush.

Everyone was coming and congratulating the couple when Mia felt a tap on her shoulder.

She turned around and saw her father and jumped in his arms.

"Oh my God daddy, what are you doing here?"

"Seantrel and your sister told me I needed to be here so I made sure to come. I couldn't miss the engagement of my baby girl."

"Daddy I'm so glad you're here, I was upset when you called and cancelled last time but I see why now."

"I know you were but I couldn't get both weekends off. You look beautiful though and congratulations. Go finish having fun, I'm not going anywhere. I'll be in town for about a week."

Mia kissed her father on the cheek before going back by Seantrel's side.

The remainder of the evening went great with the couple. They danced and talked with Seantrel's family and friends. Mia saw Ashley there but since Ashley didn't get out of pocket with her she kept her distance away from her. After all she was the one with the ring so nothing else mattered to her. She was the one that Seantrel was ready to spend the rest of his life with.

Seantrel went home and made love to Mia for the first time as his fiancé for most of the night until they both passed out. Seantrel's 27th birthday is one that he would never forget because that was the day that he made one of the biggest decisions of his life.

CHAPTER 15

Monday morning Seantrel woke up at 5:00 to get ready for work. He was getting tired of getting up so early but he had to do what he had to do. Seantrel kissed Mia on the forehead while she was still sleep and left the house.

Seantrel pulled up to his job and saw Jasmine's car sitting outside.

What the fuck she is doing here so early, he thought to himself.

Seantrel went to clock in and as soon as he walked in he saw Jasmine sitting by the time clock.

"Seantrel we need to talk."

"It's too early for this shit Jasmine."

Jasmine slid out of the way so that Seantrel could clock in then she followed him right to his office and closed the door behind them.

"Jasmine what do you want?"

"You know what I want. How could you go and propose to that bitch after you just finished fucking me almost three weeks ago?"

"First of all watch your mouth, secondly easily, that's been my woman from the beginning. I don't know why you thought I was playing when I said she wasn't going anywhere."

"Seantrel I hate that I wasted all this time with you. I haven't been fucking with nobody else for the last four months but you."

Seantrel shook his head at Jasmine; he could never understand how a lot of chicks claimed to only be with him when they knew he was already in a committed relationship.

"Jasmine what do you suggest I do?"

"I suggest you not marry her because I love you Seantrel," Jasmine said falling down to her knees in an attempt to unzip his pants.

"Get up, and as far as you loving me, I'm sorry that you caught feelings, now please leave my office because you're aggravating the hell out of me.

Seantrel opened his office door and went and had a seat behind his computer acting as if Jasmine was no longer standing there.

Jasmine stood there for a minute and then knocked everything off of Seantrel's desk as she cursed him out. Once she got it all out of her system she stormed out of the office.

Seantrel didn't even bother about chasing behind her. He just picked up everything and placed it back on his desk. He was just happy that it was only two other people that came in that early and their office was all the way on the other side of the building.

Seantrel knew he was going to have to do something about Jasmine quick because she was going to be more of a problem then he thought and he wasn't about to let anything or anyone ruin what he had going on with Mia and he definitely didn't want her stressed out while she was pregnant.

Jasmine stormed to her car talking to herself the entire time. She was mad that she allowed herself to fall full Seantrel but she couldn't help it. Who wouldn't fall in love with a man like Seantrel? He was handsome, good in bed, and financially stable. He was even nice to her in the beginning. She thought Seantrel would be like all the other men that she dated. Once she gave them a shot of head she had their minds gone and ready to move her in and take care of her but Seantrel wasn't having it all.

Jasmine knew she needed to figure out what to do because she was determined to have Seantrel in her life one way or another even it meant finding out Mia's information and contacting her about the relationship between her and Seantrel.

Jasmine felt that if she couldn't have Seantrel then nobody else would. She just needed to find out a way to implement her plan so that she could get the information that she needed.

CHAPTER 16

Mia set in the break room on the phone with LaShon during her lunch break.

"Girl that ring is freaking gorgeous that Seantrel got you, have you started thinking about a date yet?"

"Nah we haven't but we want to do something small and simple with the immediate family and friends."

"That's what's up, as long as I'm the matron of honor."

"Of course, that's a-." Mia started but stopped when her other line beeped with an unidentified phone number. Mia debated on answering on the call. She hadn't heard from her mom in a while and last time she called her phone was off so she figured it was probably her.

"Hey, let me take this call then I'm gone call you back."

"Alright," Mia said hanging up.

Mia clicked over to the other line and answered the phone.

"Hello," Mia said into the phone.

"Oh, so this is still your phone."

Mia rolled her eyes in the top of her head. "What do you want Dante?"

"What the fuck do you mean what I want? I'm home and I want what belongs to me."

"Dante I don't belong to you anymore, I've moved on."

"Fuck that, I already told you to get that shit out your system before I got home."

Mia wasn't in the mood to go back and forth with Dante so she hung up the phone on him and added that phone number to her call block list.

Mia finished up her lunch and then went back to finish up her work. She'd just finish her call with LaShon during her drive home.

The remainder of Mia's work day was a drag. Dante was texting her back and forth from different numbers and kept calling her phone. She knew she was going to have to talk to Seantrel and tell him what was going on once she got home. She couldn't let Dante jeopardize what she and Seantrel had then to make matters worse she was having morning sickness. She couldn't understand why it was called morning sickness if I went on all day.

Mia gathered her things and left work to head home. She dialed LaShon's number because she needed her help and opinion before she actually sat down and talked to Seantrel.

"Hello," LaShon answered.

"Girl, tell me why that was Dante that called me and his ass is home now."

"So what do you plan on doing about it?"

"Nothing, I told him that I was happy with Seantrel and he needs to leave me alone."

99

"So are you going to finally tell Seantrel about Dante?"

"Yeah, I don't have much of a choice since I'm about to marry him. I just hope Dante don't start no extra bullshit."

LaShon took a deep breath before speaking into the phone.

"Mia I hate to say I told you so but I did. I told you a long time ago that you needed to tell Seantrel what was going on, now you about to let the shit come back and bite you in the ass."

Mia took the phone off her ear and looked at it before putting the phone back to her ear.

"LaShon I didn't call you to be ridiculed I called you because I wanted my best friend's opinion on how to handle this situation but I guess I called the wrong number," Mia said before hanging up the phone on LaShon.

Mia was beyond pissed, never in their friendship had they ridiculed each other, pointed fingers at one another or played the "I told you so game." They were always there for each other for the most part so Mia had the slightest clue of what was going on with LaShon but at this point she really didn't give a fuck nor have the time to deal with it.

Mia took a few deep breaths then called Mianca's phone. She knew that was the one person in this world that would never judge her or condemn her no matter what.

"Hey baby sis," Mianca answered.

"Hey hunny, how are you?" Mia asked trying to sound a little happier then what she really was.

Mianca instantly picked up the tension in Mia's voice.

"Everything's good over here now you tell me what's going on over there."

Mia let out a light chuckle, "you can always tell when something is going on with me even over the phone. How do you do that?"

"Because you're my sister and that's my job to protect you and make sure that everything is alright with you so spill the beans."

Mia couldn't help but smile at her sister's words.

Mia explained everything to Mianca about her situation with Dante and what had been going on with her the last few months. She even told her about the conversation that she had just had with LaShon.

Mianca thought about her words carefully before responding to her sister.

"It seems like you got yourself caught up in a situation by not telling Seantrel from the beginning but it's never too late to right your wrongs. You need to tell Seantrel everything that you just told me. If he really loves you the way that he says he does then everything will be fine. You have to remember that no relationship is perfect and they all have their ups and downs."

"I just don't want him mad at me Mianca. I really didn't think it would be that important since I already had broken things off with Dante."

"That doesn't matter and you can't make decisions for Seantrel. He's his own person just as you are yours. Just go home and cook your man a meal and sit down and talk to him over dinner."

Mia knew what Mianca was saying was the truth. She let her doubts towards what she thought Dante would do over cloud her judgment of keeping things 100 between her and her future husband. Mia twirled her engagement ring around on her finger for a second.

"Mianca thank you for the advice, but what do I do about this LaShon situation?"

"LaShon has been your best friend since forever so I'm sure that it's not a big deal. Maybe she was already having a bad day but if it bothers you that much then you needs to talk to her once you take care of this situation. We both know life is too short to dwell on the small shit, especially the shit that we can control."

"You are so right about that but I'm home now, I love you and I'll call you later on to let you know how everything went."

"Alright, I love you too," Mianca said before hanging up.

Mianca walked in the house and Seantrel was on the couch sleeping.

She placed her things on the table and then walked over and kissed Seantrel on the forehead.

Seantrel smiled in his sleep then turned onto his side.

Mia smiled back as if he could see her before she went in the kitchen to start dinner. She was keeping it simple today with rice, chicken and mixed vegetables.

When the food was ready and the table was set Mia went and woke Seantrel up.

"Hey baby," Seantrel said while pulling Mia down on him.

"Hey baby," Mia responded while placing a luscious kiss on Mia's lips.

"Come on and eat," Mia said trying to stand up.

Seantrel sat at the table and saw the food that Mia prepared. He knew that he was making the right decision about marrying her. She made sure that she had dinner ready for him every day of the week and breakfast on the weekends. She even made his lunch and ironed his clothes for him for work faithfully.

"Everything looks good as usual my love, how was your day," Seantrel asked?

"Long," Mia said with a laugh.

"Yeah mine too; I might have to fire someone soon."

"Oh no, I know how much you hate to even have to discipline your workers since you were just on the same level as them two months ago."

"Yeah but that's neither here nor there. Why was your day so long," Seantrel asked trying to change the subject? He didn't want to talk to Mia about Jasmine. He did some trifling shit but he wasn't comfortable talking to Mia about a woman he was just fucking a few weeks ago.

"Well there's something that I wasn't up front with you about when we first met," Mia said nervously.

Seantrel put his fork down and sat all the way up in his seat. From the look that was on Mia's face he could tell that this wasn't going to be good.

Mia saw that Seantrel wasn't about to say anything so she continued.

"There's this guy name Dante that I was involved with. He was locked up when I met you but we were in a relationship up until that point."

"Hold on, so are you telling me that you have a man?"

"No I'm not, I broke up with him officially when I went out on that first date with you and things weren't good for us when he went to jail anyway."

"So why are you all of a sudden telling me now?"

"Because he called me today and told me that he was home and he was coming for what was rightfully his."

Seantrel sat there with a confused look on his face before he realized what Mia meant when she said Dante was coming for what was rightfully his.

"Do you want to be with that nigga?"

"Of course not, I'm where I want to be. I would have been told you if I knew that he were going to start acting crazy once he got home,"

Seantrel stood up from his seat and walked over to Mia and hugged her.

"There's no reason to cry ma, everything is good and we're good, I'm not mad at you," Seantrel said truthfully.

Technically Mia hadn't done anything wrong and what he was doing was far worse then what Mia had just told him and he knew she meant no harm by withholding the information. But he did know what thing that he better not

104

catch Dante anywhere near Mia or he was going to beat his ass for approaching Mia with that bullshit after he knew that they were in a relationship now.

Mia and Seantrel finished their dinner and then relaxed for the remainder of the evening.

Mia sent Mianca a text message letting her know that everything went great and she decided to let the LaShon situation go. She blamed it on her hormones.

Mia kissed Seantrel on the lips before heading upstairs so that she could get ready for bed.

Seantrel waited until he heard the shower running then pulled out his phone.

"Yeah," the caller answered on the first ring.

"What the fuck are you doing calling my fiancé?"

Dante looked down at the phone to check the number again and let out a chuckle.

"That was my bitch before you decided to wife her. Nobody told you to go and fall in love with what belonged to me."

"We both know that I didn't know she was yours and let her tell it that shit was over with before I stuck my dick in her."

"Mia was mine and will always be mine. I was her first love rather you like it or not now get off my phone with that bullshit," Dante said before hanging up the phone on Seantrel.

Seantrel threw his phone across the couch and closed his eyes thinking about the day that he found out that Dante was Mia's boyfriend.

Seantrel was at work finishing up when his co-worker as well as friend from the block Antonio walked over to him.

"You know that bitch that you been fucking with is Dante's girlfriend right."

"What Dante are you talking about?"

"You know Dante from the block, the one that Steven did work for off and on."

"Oh ok, I remember him now, fuck him, I been asked him to not have my brother work for him but he ignored it. So now he'll just have to hear about me fucking his bitch then."

"Well word on the block is he knows all about y'all and once he gets home he taking her back and your brother will be back on the corner nickel and diming for him."

"Yeah, well pass the word on that I ain't worried about his ass and his bitch will be calling me daddy before the night out. As far as my brother goes ain't shit I can't do about that."

That same day Seantrel vowed to make sure Mia would never want to go back to Dante once he got home.

He started to wine and dine her up until the point that he convinced her to move in with him.

Seantrel opened his eyes after he realized the flaw that was in his plan. He never had intended on falling in love with Mia for real. Now there was no way in hell he was going to let Dante come and take his place now that his own heart was actually on the line.

Seantrel had to think of a way to get Mia to marry him sooner than next year. He knew once she was his wife there was no way that she would change her mind or stray back to Dante.

CHAPTER 17

Mia sat in front of the mirror and applied her makeup. She could see the stress lines that were forming in her beautiful face and she wasn't happy about it at all. Over the past couple of months Mia couldn't tell rather she was coming or going. She felt like she was stressed to the max. She was just happy that the stress wasn't affecting her pregnancy. Dante wouldn't leave well enough alone and against her better judgment she allowed Seantrel to push her wedding day up to today.

Mia knew that she wanted to marry Seantrel but she didn't understand what the rush was for. It seemed like once she told Seantrel about Dante all he did was talk about them getting married like he was doing it to make sure she didn't change her mind.

"So what do y'all think? Do you think I should've told Seantrel that we should still wait until next year to get married?" Mia asked Mianca and LaShon.

"Well I already told you that the whole situation seemed suspect especially since he asked you to move the date up to today the same night that you told him Dante was home. It's like he got to prove something. Plus didn't you say that someone has been calling his phone private? The only person that calls and plays on niggas phones is a pissed off bitch that he stopped fucking with but she still wants the dick."

Mia let out a loud sigh. She was tired of LaShon trying to convince her that Seantrel was straying. Seantrel wasn't doing anything that he wasn't supposed to do in Mia's book. He came home every night; he was still fucking her, still taking her out and providing for their home. He never gave her a reason to question him so she definitely wasn't going to nag him just because of a few petty private calls.

"LaShon gone somewhere with that bullshit, she already looks stressed enough," Mianca said before rolling her eyes then standing up from the couch to waddle over to her sister.

"Baby girl you look beautiful and you don't have anything to worry about. "Everyone's nerves go on edge the day of their wedding. If you didn't have those butterflies then something would be wrong. Seantrel already told you why he wanted to get married now and I think it's sweet."

Seantrel told Mia that he wanted to marry her before the baby got here the right way. So today they were just having a small wedding and a reception then they were going to the Bahamas for five days for their honeymoon. Mia could understand the reasoning behind it and agreed to it because as far as she was concerned they could have gone to the justice of peace. Mia just didn't want it to be for the wrong reasons then next thing she knew she would be a single divorced mother at the age of 22.

LaShon rolled her eyes at Mia and Mianca's conversation. She couldn't understand how they could be so naïve but then again she kind of could since neither of them had ever had their hearts broken as an adult. Mianca had been with Isaiah who was the nice and innocent guy and Mia was with Dante before Seantrel and she was the one that broke up with him.

LaShon knew for a fact though that Dante was fucking other bitches because she saw it with her own eyes but when she got to the point when she was finally going to tell Mia he got locked up so it was no longer important. That was the main reason why she was happy that Mia had met

Seantrel. She knew that it would be a good distraction to keep Mia's mind away from Dante but she never expected Mia to fall in love, get pregnant and married within 15 months of being with the nigga.

LaShon saw niggas like Seantrel all the time and knew that he was up to no good and had her girl's nose wide open. There was no wrong in Mia's eyes toward Seantrel. Mia could walk in on Seantrel fucking a bitch and Mia would close her eyes and walk back out like nothing had just happened.

LaShon hated that her friend was so naïve and gullible but right now there wasn't anything she could do about it except give her a shoulder to cry on when her perfect little world started to crumble to pieces.

"Look I'm sorry Mia; I'm not trying to stress you out. You know I got a bad habit of sticking my foot in my mouth but you know that I love you and you looking stunning," said LaShon.

Mia did look stunning in her cream off the shoulder wedding dress. It was simple but yet elegant. It hid her small protruding stomach just as she wanted it to.

"It's all good LaShon, you're my best friend and I know that you only have my best interest at heart."

There was a knock at the door and Mia looked down at her phone and saw that it was time for them to leave out for the ceremony.

Mianca, Mia and LaShon walked out into the hallways of the "Sabre Room" where Mia and Seantrel's wedding would take place. There was going to be a simple ceremony outside and the reception followed directly inside of the hall upstairs.

Mia listened as "Angel of Mine" by Monica played in the background.

Stephanie, LaShon and Mianca started marching out and Antonio, Steven and Isaiah met them half way and walked them to the front of aisle.

The song switched over and "Hear and Now" by Luther Vandross was playing as their flower girls walked down the aisle. Their flower girls were Stephanie's daughter Shantaye and Mia's little cousin Gabrielle.

The girls looked absolutely adorable as they kissed the flowers before they dropped them on the ground.

Lastly "All My life" by K-Ci and JoJo played which was Mia's que to get ready and walk down the aisle.

Mia's father walked up to her and kissed her on the cheek before pulling the veil over her face. "You look absolutely gorgeous," he said into her ear.

Mia smiled from ear to ear. No matter how many men complimented her it never compared to when her father did it.

Mia walked down the aisle with her father and admired the beautiful scenery. You could see the pond directly behind the reverend and wedding party. It wasn't anything major but it was still beautiful to her and 50 of their closes friends and family were in attendance.

Mia got closer to the front and looked over at the empty seat where her mother should have been sitting and took a deep breath to keep from crying. She went to visit her mother numerous times and tried to talk her into coming to the wedding but it never worked. Each time Melissa had a new excuse of why she couldn't attend her youngest child wedding. But Mia shouldn't have expected more being that they almost had to drag her out of the house to attend Maurice's funeral.

Mia brushed it off once her father released her arm and allowed Seantrel's arm to inner twine with hers.

Mia shook all of her issues off and knew that she was making the right decision. At that point it could have been just his parents, Mianca, LaShon and her father and she would have been just fine with it because she was about to marry the man of her dreams and there wasn't anything that anyone could do about it.

Mia and Seantrel shared their vows with one another and then said I do. Mia and Seantrel kissed for the first time as Mr. and Mrs. Anderson and there was a lot of applause and whistles from the crowd.

Mia and Seantrel had a blast at their wedding reception and that day was one of the happiest days of their lives. They waited as everyone began leaving the reception before they dipped out so that they could go home. They were staying at home that night and taking a flight out the next morning for Hawaii.

Seantrel had just finished making love to his wife when his cell phone started vibrating. He looked down at the phone wondering who would be calling him the night of his wedding day.

"Hello," Seantrel said as he eased out of bed to go downstairs.

"So you went on and married that bitch for real."

"I told you I was going to marry her. I didn't go spend 7k on a ring for it to just look pretty on her finger."

"Well can I see you tonight?

"Hell no but I'll give you a call once I get back from my honeymoon. Please refrain from calling me because my phone will be turned off," Seantrel said to Ashley before hanging up the phone.

Seantrel couldn't believe Ashley had just called him looking for some dick on his wedding day. *These bitches don't have any respect* he thought.

CHAPTER 18

The next morning Mia and Seantrel were up and out of the house 7 A.M. so that they could make their 10:00 flight. Mia and Seantrel had both flew before but this were their first time flying internationally and this was the longest flight that either of them had ever flown.

By the time they made it to Hawaii Mia's body was aching and her legs felt like putty from sitting in one place for so long. Seantrel and Mia admired the beauty of Hawaii during their taxi ride to their hotel. Everything looked so bright and beautiful where they were staying at. They had an ocean view room that looked magnificent from their bed.

"Seantrel I love this," Mia said while tonguing him down.

"This as in the room or me," Seantrel asked jokingly.

"Right now it's a tie between the two," Mia answered honestly.

"Oh really, I can't be tying with a room so I'm going to have to make you love me more."

Seantrel undressed Mia and then himself before leading her to the shower. They took a nice steamy shower. Mia couldn't tell what felt better at that moment between Seantrel's hands and the hot water hitting up against her body. He washed her body from head to toe and then grabbed the shampoo and gently massaged in into her scalp. Mia allowed a seductive moan to escape her lips. She loved when Seantrel washed her hair for her. His muscular hands felt so much better than any chick at the shop who ever washed it.

Once Seantrel finished washing Mia's hair he grabbed one of the huge dry towels and dried her hair and body off before leading her to the bed where he laid down and allowed her to lay her head upon his chest.

Seantrel gently rubbed his fingers up and down Mia's spine. With every touch she felt a chill run through her body. The tips of his fingers felt like silk against her moist skin. The way his hands felt up against her body at that moment was unexplainable. His hands felt so good against her body but she couldn't wait to feel his tongue sop up every crease of her flesh. Just the thought of it caused Mia to squeeze her legs together a little tighter.

The chemistry that they shared made their hearts beat as one. All Mia could hear was boom, boom, boom, boom while her head lay gently across his rock hard chest. He rubbed his fingers through her soft curls and gently massaged her scalp.

"You look so beautiful and smell so delicious right now. I just want to eat you up," Seantrel said in his husky voice.

Mia looked up into his big beautiful brown eyes and gave him one of the sincerest smiles that she could muster up. The smile was so genuine and delicate that he could feel it from his heart to the tip of his toes.

Mia opened her mouth to speak but Seantrel gently placed a finger to her lips and whispered "shhhhhhh". His luscious lips grazed the tip of her earlobe causing her to shudder.

Seantrel repositioned himself where he could hover over Mia. He placed one of her voluptuous breast into his mouth and nibbled on them. He sucked on them hard enough to cause a little pain. The pain sent a surge of pleasure through her body.

Seantrel gently flipped Mia onto her stomach and reached over into the bowl that was on the nightstand which contained a variety of fruit. He bit into one of the sweetest and juiciest pieces of fruit. Some of the juice slid between his succulent lips and reached his chin. He took the remainder of the pineapples and made a trail from the top of her neck down to the crack of her ass.

Mia felt Seantrel replace the fruit with the tip of his tongue. His tongue slithered down her back like a snake. "Ahhhhhhhh" a soft moan had escaped Mia's lips without her permission.

Seantrel lifted Mia legs up into a kneeling position where she could be on all fours. She arched her back as she felt his tongue enter her love canal. He licked and slurped, licked and slurped, and lick and slurped some more. He licked from her pussy to her ass.

Seantrel flipped Mia onto her back and placed both of her thick thighs over his shoulders. He kissed the inside of the right thigh first then the inside of the left one. He used two of his fingers to open up her pussy lips.

Seantrel licked around the outside of her lips then French kissed her pearl tongue. Mia could have sworn that her husband was heaven sent when she felt one then two of his thick fingers inside of her. He worked his two fingers in and out of Mia while he continued to suck on her clit like it was a sweet nectarine.

He removed his fingers from her pussy and stuck one inside of her anus. Mia heart started racing and her body began to convulse. "Ohhhhhh…. Shiiiittttttt, I'm cummmm-," Mia started to say but her words got caught in her throat as

116

she felt the biggest orgasm she had ever had rush through her body. Mia tried to remove her legs from his shoulders but she couldn't.

"Hold on baby….God…what the fuck…" Mia tried to protest. Her pussy was extra sensitive as Seantrel continued to suck on it like it was a Popsicle on a hot August day. Mia began to squirm which only caused him to suck harder and get an even stronger grip on her legs. Seantrel continued to lick and slurp on her love button until he felt her squirt in his mouth.

Seantrel positioned himself so that he could enter her love cave. She wrapped her legs around his waist and welcomed every inch of his curve into her. She loved the way he handed her the D. It was long and hard sensual strokes. "Hmmmm…. Damn right there," Mia moaned out into ecstasy. He grabbed a fist full of her hair with one hand and held onto the back of her neck with the other one. He was hitting just the right spots and she could feel her body shake sporadically onto another mind blowing orgasm. It was like Seantrel was taking her on that rollercoaster ride again. Every time it seemed like she was about to hit the bottom there was a pause, bringing her back to reality.

Mia's body felt like it was getting cramped up under Seantrel so they traded places. Mia climbed on top of Seantrel's rod and glided up and down in a circular motion. When she felt herself on the verge of another mind blowing orgasm she sped up the speed like she was riding a horse at the Kentucky Derby. Seantrel let out a groan and grabbed a handful of her ass. Mia knew that she had him just where she wanted. He was ready to bust that nut.

Mia hopped up and before Seantrel could protest she placed his dick in her mouth. She glided her tongue up and down the shaft before deep throating it. Mia could feel his dick against her tonsils and his balls hitting up against her chin. It was now Seantrel's turn to cum in her mouth. Mia refused to stop until she felt every drop go down her throat.

"Damn girl, hold on," Seantrel protested. Mia was sucking away while his dick head was extra sensitive just from her tongue grazing up against it.

Seantrel grabbed a handful of Mia's wet hair and pulled her head up. Mia stopped sucking and burst out into laughter. Seantrel could never take what he dished out. He never stopped when Mia told him to but as soon as she did it to him he used his strength as his advantage.

"Oh so you think it's funny huh? Ok, give me one sec."

Seantrel snatched Mia up like she was a rag doll and made her sit on his face. He had a death grip around her waist as he slurped away at her sweet pussy. Mia rode Seantrel's face until she felt a mind blowing orgasm approach. The tighter Mia's pussy contracted the faster Seantrel sucked until he felt Mia's juices sliding down the side of face. He lifted her up and smiled as he saw the glazed look in her eyes.

Mia laid next to Seantrel and as soon as her head touched his shoulder she was passed out instantly with Seantrel following right behind her. Between the sex and the flight they both were exhausted and slept through the entire night.

CHAPTER 19

Mia and Seantrel had a blissful honeymoon in Hawaii and neither of them wanted to return to the real world but they both had plenty of work that needed to be done once they made it back to Chicago.

Mia and Seantrel stayed nestled up together for the first day that they returned home. They kept it as no cell phones and no communication from the outside world. The next morning Mia and Seantrel was up bright and early so that Mia could go get her ultrasound done and then they both were off to work.

Mia was nervous and excited about finding out what she was having. She would finally be able to go baby shopping and start to pick out names as well. Mia or Seantrel really didn't care what the sex of the baby was as long as he or she was healthy.

Mia laid flat on her back as her ultrasound was being performed. The gel was still cold but she loved the site of seeing her baby on the screen.

"So what do the lucky couple want to have," asked the ultrasound technician.

"It really doesn't matter as long as it's healthy," stated Seantrel.

The ultrasound tech took a few pictures of Mia's stomach before speaking again.

"So I guess that means you don't want to know the sex", she said jokingly.

"Don't play like that," Mia said laughing.

"Ok, ok, ok, I see mama is a little feisty. Well it looks like you will be having a boy."

"Yayyy," Mia squealed.

Seantrel was ecstatic on this inside. He was about to have a little boy that could carry his name.

Seantrel leaned down and kissed Mia on her forehead and then kissed her on her stomach not caring about the gel that was on it.

The ultrasound tech exited the room so that Mia could finish getting dressed. Once Mia and Seantrel were exiting the room she handed them a couple of the shots she got from the sonogram.

Seantrel dropped Mia off at work since they came in the same car.

"Please be on time to pick me up," Mia said before kissing Seantrel and exiting the car.

"I will, I promise," Seantrel said before pulling off.

Mia entered her job and the receptionist gave her the messages and back work that she had been missing. Mia knew that she would be busy all day because she had a week worth of work to catch up on. She was happy and relaxed though so it wouldn't be too hard for her to get it done.

Mia was sitting at her desk making calls and she was in the process of dialing another number when the operator called over the phone speaker informing her that she had a call. That was kind of weird to Mia because no one ever contacted her on the job phone. She looked at her cell phone and saw that she had no missed calls or voices mails.

"Johnson and Higgins this is Mia, how may I help you," Mia answered professionally.

"You can't help me but I can help you. Do you know where your husband is right now?"

"Excuse me," Mia said into the phone.

"You heard me; I just thought that you should know that your husband ain't who you think he is."

"Whatever, get off my line with that bull," Mia said hanging up the phone.

Mia really wanted to curse the caller out but she knew that their calls were recorded periodically so she had to keep the call as professional as possible.

Mia picked up her phone to dial Seantrel's phone number but changed her mind. She knew that there were other bitches that wanted her husband before she married him but she couldn't be mad about that. She knew she needed to trust the man that she had fell in love with and was about to spend the rest of her life with.

Mia shook the negative thoughts out of her head and got back to work. She was about 30 minutes into her work when her cell phone started vibrating. She looked down at the screen and saw her and Seantrel's wedding picture display on the screen. A huge smile crossed Mia's lips because she knew that her husband couldn't be fucking some bitch and calling her phone at the same time.

"Heeeeyy, my love," Mia sung into the phone.

"Hey baby, how's your day going so far," asked Seantrel?

"Even better now that I hear your voice." Mia chose not to give out the information from the caller. She didn't see the need to bring him any unnecessary issues.

"Ok, cool, I just wanted to call and check you. I need to get back to work but I'll try to call you before I get off, if not I'll see you at 4:00."

"Alright baby, I love you," Mia said into the phone.

"I love you too Seantrel said hanging up.

Mia leaned back in her seat and smiled. She didn't know why she ever doubted Seantrel anyway.

CHAPTER 20

"I don't know why the fuck you lying to that girl about you loving her and I still don't know why you married her ass. That should have been me," Ashley said looking up at Seantrel.

"Look I do love her and I have my reasons for marrying her. Now are we going to do this so that I can go or did you ask me to come over here so that you could nag me?"

Ashley rolled her eyes before placing Seantrel's dick back in her mouth. She didn't know why she couldn't get Seantrel out of her system. No matter how badly he treated her she always found her way right back to him and allowed him to treat her like shit. But she felt a sense that Seantrel had some type of feelings for her being that she called him this morning and he was willing to come fuck her the day after he just came back from his honeymoon.

Ashley sucked Seantrel off until he was hard and then she rolled a condom on his dick and rode him until she came. Once she came Seantrel flipped her over and rammed his dick in her from the back until he felt himself about to cum. Once he felt his balls tense up he pulled out of Ashley and took the condom off and made her suck his dick until he came in her mouth.

As quick as he came he was sticking his dick back in his boxers and pulling his pants up.

"Damn, that's all I get. Where you about to go," Ashley asked with an attitude.

"I got shit to take care of, you called and asked could I come make you cum and that's what I did. I know you got your nut off. No matter how times I stick my dick in you there's only one person that I'm willing to put in extra time and work for and that's my wife. She is the only one that's getting anything past 15 minutes or more than one nut from me. If you want anything more you better find you another nigga to come and fuck you," Seantrel said arrogantly as he grabbed his keys and walked out of her house.

Ashley looked at Seantrel and tears instantly blurred her vision. She wanted to chase after him and curse him out for treating her like she was a jump off. But when she thought about it that's really all she was being that she was fucking and chasing behind a married man.

Ashley sat on the couch and put her face in her hands trying to figure out how to get out of the situation. Her mind was telling her to tell Seantrel to fuck him and then delete his number from her phone but her heart wouldn't even allow her to get up from the couch and even yell at him

Ashley heard Seantrel's ringtone on her phone and looked over and answered it.

"Hello," she answered through sniffles.

"Look cut it out with that crying shit. Come outside and bring your car keys with you," Seantrel said angrily through the phone.

Ashley grabbed her keys and stepped outside of her apartment. She walked to Seantrel and she could see him punching the car and yelling at somebody on the phone.

"If I find out you had anything to do with this I'm fucking your ass up," Seantrel yelled before hanging up the phone.

Ashley was about to ask Seantrel what was wrong until she saw that his car had four flat tires and somebody had keyed the words male whore into his car.

Ashley laughed on the inside because that just proved to her that she wasn't the only one Seantrel was creeping on Mia with and his ways were finally catching up with him. She really wanted to know how he was going to explain this situation to his precious wife being that his car was parked outside of her apartment complex.

Seantrel looked up at Ashley and saw the smug list on her face. "Don't you say shit," he yelled at her.

Seantrel looked down at his phone and knew that he wasn't going to have enough time to wait on triple A to come and fix his tires and have enough time to go pick Mia up from work on time.

"Fuck," Seantrel yelled as he punched the side of the car.

Seantrel called Antonio's phone to see if he could come and pick him up from Ashley's place.

"Hello," Antonio answered.

"Hey man, I need you to come and pick me up from Ashley's house."

"What the fuck are you doing there?"

"I'll explain everything to you when you get here. Just come on, I'm already outside."

"Alright, I'll be there in about 20 minutes."

Seantrel stuck his phone back in his pocket and tried to think of an excuse to tell Mia. There was no way in hell he could allow her to see his car that way.

Seantrel dialed Steven's number and then walked away from Ashley so that she wouldn't hear his phone conversation.

"Yo, what's up bro?"

"Hey man, I need you to come to Ashley's place and sit with Triple A while they fix my tires. Somebody flattened all my tires and keyed my car while I was in her house."

"What the fuck were you doing with that bitch? Do you think it was Mia?"

"Nah, Mia is at work that's why I can't stay here and wait. I need to go pick her up and go to the house and get her car. I'll have Antonio come pick you up after he drop us off at home then I'll be back to pick you up."

"Alright, I'm at the house. You need to quit it with this dumb shit though. You just married a beautiful woman who's about to have your baby and you keep sticking your dick in that nasty bitch. You got to do better Seantrel, for real," Steven said into the phone before hanging up on Seantrel.

Seantrel couldn't help but shake his head. He knew that he needed to get it together for real when his younger sibling started giving him advice. Steven may have not done what he was supposed to as far as doing right in the streets and getting a legit job but he did make sure to treat women with respect and like the queens that they were. He was never into fucking multiple women if he was in a serious relationship. They were never raised that way which was one of the main reasons why no one could understand why Seantrel did the shit that he did.

Seantrel made a call to AAA and by the time he hung up with them Antonio was pulling up.

"Aye Ashley, Steve will be here in a little while to sit with my car until AAA gets here."

"Alright, give me your keys."

"Nah, I'm going to give them to Antonio and he'll give them to Steven," Seantrel said before walking away.

Seantrel didn't trust leaving his keys with Ashley because there was no telling if her sneaky ass would try to plant some shit in his car. He was already in enough trouble as it is.

Seantrel got in the car with Antonio and he could feel the hole that was burning into the side of his head from Antonio's eyes.

"Look, before you say it, I know I fucked up."

"You damn right you fucked up. You my homey so of course I got your back but I also got to give it to you straight. You just got back from your honeymoon yesterday and you fucking another bitch already today. That's wrong on so many levels. Your ass gone wake up one day to an empty house because this shit is going to catch up with your ass one day."

Seantrel sat there with his head back and listened to Antonio lecture him. He had never done the one woman thing before so he wasn't too sure of how to do it now. He loved Mia but the main reason that he married her was because she was pregnant and he didn't want her with another man. He wanted to be able to raise his child in a two parent home the same way he was.

Antonio pulled up to Mia's job 30 minutes later and parked so that Seantrel could get out and go get Mia.

"I'll be right back," Seantrel said as he exited the car.

Seantrel went to the front desk and signed in before heading to the back where Mia's cubicle was located.

Mia was sitting on a phone call with her back turned towards the people. Seantrel crept up on her and placed his hands over her eyes.

"Guess who," he said playfully.

"Uhm," Mia said acting as if she had to think about who it was behind her. "Is it my loving husband?" Mia asked as she hung up and spun around to look at his handsome face.

"The one and only baby, you ready to get out of here?"

"Yeah, just let me log out my computer and grab my bags."

Mia logged out and Seantrel lifted her from her chair and embraced her in a hug causing her to instantly get a whiff of his body.

There was a strong pungent sent of a woman's cheap body spray on him with a mixture of sweat.

Mia instantly removed her arms from around Seantrel and walked with him outside. Mia looked around for Seantrel's car but it was nowhere to be found. She followed him to Antonio's car and was about to say something but then she saw Antonio in the car and changed her mind. She didn't want to get him involved in their business.

The entire ride to Seantrel's and Mia's home was quiet except for the music playing in the back ground. Mia was starting to believe what LaShon had been telling her and maybe the bitch that called her phone was actually the one that he had just left. All kinds of crazy thoughts were going through Mia's head.

As soon as they pulled up to the house Mia jumped out the car without even saying goodbye to Antonio.

"Man she is pissed; do you need me to stay?"

"Nah, I'm good, just make sure to pick up Steven and give him the keys to my car. Tell him if AAA gets there and finish before I get there to just take the car to my parent's house."

"Yeah nigga, cause it don't look like you gone be able to get back out of the house today," Antonio said laughing.

"Whatever nigga, I'm a grown ass man and I pay every bill in this bitch. Her ass works just because she wants to say that she ain't depending on any man."

Antonio looked at Seantrel again and burst out into laughter as he pulled off.

Seantrel walked into the house and before he had a chance to close the door Mia was yelling at him.

"Where the fuck have you been and where is your car?"

"Baby calm down, I was at work and Steven has my car. He came to the job to get my car and someone split my tires while he was at some bitch house thinking he was driving someone else's car."

"Whatever, you fucking smell like another bitch. You could've at least got your ass in the shower before coming to get me," Mia said with a disgusted look on her face.

"Mia, I wasn't with no damn bitch, don't start acting insecure now that we married."

"What the fuck ever," Mia said as she walked up the stairs to their bedroom and slammed the door.

Seantrel was about to follow behind her but changed his mind and went into the hall bathroom to take a quick shower before going in the room to talk to her.

Seantrel took a quick shower and put his clothes in the laundry bag before walking into his bedroom. Mia was lying on the bed balled up and Seantrel could tell that she had been crying.

Seantrel grabbed a tank top and a pair of boxers and then climbed in bed with Mia.

"Baby please don't cry, I didn't mean to upset you and we don't need the stress for the baby."

Mia turned around on her back and looked up into Seantrel's face. She could see the guilt in his eyes and his infidelity was evident.

Her eyes instantly filled with tears again and she turned her back towards him.

Seantrel sat there quietly as he watched Mia fall asleep. Once she fell asleep Seantrel left out of the room and went downstairs to call Steven.

"Hey man, did they come yet?"

"Yeah they just finished, I'm on my way home now."

"Can you just bring the car to my house? Mia's mad and I don't want to leave her at home alone right now."

"Alright, I'll be there in a little while."

Seantrel hung up the phone with Steven and walked back in the house and laid across the couch before his phone started ringing.

Seantrel answered the phone without saying anything and walked outside.

"What the fuck are you doing calling me at home?"

"I thought you were coming back."

"Nah I couldn't get away."

Seantrel heard Ashley let out a sigh. "Well can I meet you at your job tomorrow to get the money to get my hair done?"

Seantrel let out a slight chuckle from his irritation.

"Nah, I'll give the money to Steven when he gets here and you can just pick it up from my mom's house.

"Alright," Ashley said happily into the phone.

Seantrel hung up his phone and sat on the porch until Steven pulled up. Once Steven pulled up he hopped in the car and rode to his mother's house and came directly back home.

Seantrel threw his keys on the table and went back upstairs to a sleeping Mia. He undressed and snuggled up under her. He tried his best to sleep but it seemed like his thoughts were too loud for him to sleep. All this time he had never had a conscious but now it seemed like it was kicking all the way in.

Seantrel said a silent prayer asking the Lord to give him strength to do right by Mia and his unborn son.

2 ½ YEARS LATER/ PRESENT DAY

CHAPTER 21

Mia found herself laying in bed alone for yet another night. It was almost three in the morning and Seantrel still hadn't found his way back in the house.

Seantrel's and Mia's marriage was having their ups and downs. Seantrel was an excellent father to their 1 ½ year old son Seantrel Jr. and their 6 month old daughter Sennett. If only he was half as good of a husband everything would be perfect between them two. Seantrel got to the point where he would stop answering his phone when he was out if Mia called. The only thing he was consistent with was coming home for dinner and making sure he tucked SJ in before he left his ass right back out the house.

Mianca tried to convince Mia to divorce Seantrel but the love that Mia had for him and the love that he showed towards his kids wouldn't allow her to do it. She wanted more than anything for her kids to be raised in a stable two parent home. She wanted them to have everything that she never had.

Mia had finally fallen asleep when she felt the sheet being tugged from off of her. She looked over at the clock and saw that it was 5:03 A.M. She just shook her head and rolled over on her side. She was at the point that she didn't even bothering about asking him where he had been. She got a whiff of Seantrel as he stripped down to his boxers and climbed under the covers with her.

"Well at least you decided to shower before bringing your ass home this time."

"Mia do not start this bullshit with me. I'm not having this shit with you tonight now take your ass back to bed."

Tears threatened to escape Mia's eyes but she didn't allow them to fall. She was tired of crying over Seantrel. If she ever wanted things to be right she would have to be the one to fix it. After all Seantrel could only do what Mia allowed him to do.

The next morning Mia woke up and was out of the house with the kids while Seantrel was still passed out in bed.

Mia dropped SJ and Sennett off at daycare then she called her friend Donovan. They had stayed in touch with each other after they graduated and he had been helping her with the issues she was having in her marriage.

"Hey beautiful," Donovan said over the phone.

"Hey Don," Mia said with a smile. Donovan knew how to make her smile and still make her always feel beautiful even when she didn't think so. "Why do you sound so stressed baby girl?"

"I'm just tired; I could really use a friend right now."

"Well give me about 20 minutes then I can meet you at the Starbucks up the street from your job."

"Alright," Mia said before hanging up.

Mia was already down the street from the Starbucks so she found a parking spot and then went and found a table that was sitting outside of Starbucks.

Mia called LaShon's phone and just as always it would ring and then go to voicemail. It was at the point where LaShon no longer answered Mia's phone calls or returned them. Granted she was upset that Mia was putting up with Seantrel still but he was her husband so what did she expect from her. LaShon was her best friend and was supposed to always be there for her through the good and the bad.

Mia was going to leave a voicemail but didn't see a purpose. Mia was at the point that she was tired of everything. She was emotionally and physically drained with her marriage, her friendship with LaShon, and even her relationship with Mianca was rocky because every time she talked to her she was trying to convince Mia to leave Seantrel and come live with her.

The only good things were her kids and the friendship she had with Donovan but she wasn't sure if that could be considered a good thing because she had deep feelings for Donovan that a married woman should never have for another man. They never crossed the line because Mia was married and wanted to remain faithful even though she knew Seantrel wasn't shit. Donovan couldn't do anything but respect Mia's wishes. He knew once she had enough she would leave that nigga and he'd be there waiting for her with open arms.

Mia was looking down at her phone checking her email when she heard the chair in front of her slide back.

Mia looked up and a huge smile spread across her lips. Donovan was just as handsome as he was three years ago if not more. He was clean shaven and was rocking a short fade now. His dark skin was so smooth that Mia imagined that he tasted like a Hershey's bar she wanted to lick every inch of him. Every man that she had ever dated was light skinned but she was always told that chocolate melted in your mouth. Just the thought of it made Mia have to clench her legs together tighter.

"Mia, Mia did you hear me," Donovan called out?

"Oh, yes, I mean I'm sorry, what did you say Don?"

Donovan shook his head at Mia, "you must have really been thinking hard that you didn't hear anything I had just said."

"If only you knew," Mia mumbled under breath.

"What was that you said," asked Donovan. He heard what Mia said but he wanted to see if she would repeat it.

"Oh, nothing at all, it wasn't important," Mia said blushing slightly from embarrassment.

Donovan reached over and grabbed Mia by the hand. "Well when you're ready to talk about that non important situation just let me know."

Mia was at a loss for words so she only nodded her head up and down.

"So what had you in so much of a funk this morning?" Donovan asked trying to change the subject.

"The usual, Seantrel came in for dinner but as soon as SJ was tucked in he was out the door 15 minutes after that and didn't come back home until 5:00 this morning and then had a nerve to get an attitude because I said something to him.

"Mia I keep telling you that you don't have to put up with that shit. You're too young for that. You're a beautiful 25 year old woman."

"That's the thing though, I don't feel beautiful. I have never been this size in my life. My own husband doesn't even think I'm beautiful anymore. I just feel that if I can lose this weight then he'll do right by me," Mia said sadly.

Donovan's heart instantly melted when he heard Mia speak those words. He hated that over time her self-esteem for herself had decreased instantly. He remembered when he first met Mia no one couldn't tell her that she wasn't the most gorgeous woman in the room.

Mia had gained 45 pounds during her pregnancy with Sennett but was only able to lose 20 of those pounds so she was carrying an extra 25 pounds. She wasn't sloppy with the weight. Her hips and thighs had gotten bigger and her stomach wasn't as flat as it used to be and her arms were a little thicker.

In Donovan's eyes she was still perfect. He found nothing wrong with a woman having a little meat on her bones. He grew up with nothing but thick women in his family so he loved the beauty of a woman no matter what her size was.

"Sweetheart look at me, you are extremely beautiful, beauty isn't determined by a size or pound it is determined by what's on the inside. But beauty is also determined on how the person feels about themselves. If you don't feel that you're beautiful baby girl then how can you expect anyone else to think that you are? So if you want to lose the weight to make you love yourself more and not because of your ignorant ass husband then I will help you. You can start going to the gym with me whenever you have free time."

"I like that idea; I would love to work out with you, in the gym that it is."

"Baby girl you can work out with me any kind of way that you want to," Donovan said with a wink of the eye.

Mia swallowed the lump that was in her throat before they continued to talk. By the time they finished talking Mia had to hurry up so that she wouldn't be late for work.

Donovan walked Mia to her car and wrapped his muscular arms around her body. Mia took in a deep breath so that Donovan's scent could fill her nostrils. She loved the way he smelled. She always wanted to know what it was that he wore but he would never tell her. He always told her that as long as she didn't know the scent but liked it she would always come around to smell it on him.

"Thanks for coming here so early to talk to me. I really do appreciate it."

"It's no problem; I'm always a phone call away no matter the time of the day."

Mia let go from the hug first and Donovan looked her in the eyes and then kissed her on the forehead. Donovan had the look in his eyes that Seantrel use to once have for her. She would give anything to get that same look from her husband.

Mia got in her car and headed to work. As soon as she got to work and was seated at her desk her mind wouldn't allow her to focus on work. All she could think about was Seantrel. She needed to do something to fix her marriage before it was too late. After being at work for two hours Mia went to her supervisor's office and told her that she was feeling sick and was heading home.

Mia gathered her things and headed home. She didn't bother about picking up the kids because she needed the alone time with Seantrel besides the sitter was paid for up until 6:00. The closer Mia got to her home she felt like something wasn't wrong. She had a sick feeling in her stomach for real and didn't know why.

Mia drove towards her house and saw a car that looked familiar a couple of houses down but she shook her head because after all when they made one car they didn't stop making them all.

Something told Mia to drive her car around to the back and for the first time in a long time she was going to follow her intuition and do what it said so she pulled her car up to the back and got out.

Mia entered her house through the back door and dropped her keys on the kitchen counter. She stripped down to her underwear in hopes that her husband would be in a good mood by now and give her some loving. Mia pushed the door open that led to the living room and stopped right in her tracks. She couldn't believe what she was seeing. Her husband was sitting on the couch with his eyes closed and a bitch on her knees in between his legs sucking his dick.

"Seantrel what the fuck is going on in here," Mia yelled!

Seantrel opened his eyes and looked at Mia as if he was pissed off that she had interrupted his nut. The chick that was sucking Seantrel's dick lifted her head up and looked as if her soul had left her body.

Mia stood there frozen in place because she could not believe her eyes or her ears. She knew that this had to be some kind of sick joke.

Mia instantly felt sick and ran into the kitchen and threw up in the sink.

She had always known about Seantrel's infidelities but she dealt with it because of their kids and he was an excellent provider but this shit took things to another level. She couldn't believe how disrespectful Seantrel was being. She was even more hurt by the chick that he decided to fuck in their home.

By the time Seantrel decided to go in the kitchen and chase after Mia she was stumbling to pull her jeans up as the tears fell from her eyes. She couldn't get her clothes fixed fast enough so that she could get out of that house.

Seantrel walked over to Mia and wiped the tears from her eyes.

Mia looked up at Seantrel and gave him a look of disgust. The nigga didn't even have the decency to put his pants back on.

"Don't ever put your hands on me again in your life."

Seantrel ignored Mia and reached for her again and before he knew it Mia had slapped the shit out of him.

Seantrel reached his hand up to grab Mia but she grabbed the knife off the counter. He lifted his hands to surrender and exited the kitchen as quick as he walked in.

Mia grabbed her keys to leave the house but changed her mind. She dropped the keys on the counter and stormed towards the living room with the knife. Seantrel had started this game but Mia was going to be the one to end it.

Mia rushed into the living room and was surprised to see LaShon's dumb ass still standing there.

"What the fuck are you still doing in my house," Mia asked LaShon?

"I thought that we could talk about this Mia."

Mia looked between LaShon and Seantrel and got even madder. She looked at the knife that was in her hands but then at the pictures of her children that were on the wall and knew that neither of them was worth her spending time away from her kids so she dropped the knife and rushed LaShon.

Mia slapped the taste out of LaShon's mouth. "You were supposed to be my motherfucking best friend and you in here sucking and fucking my husband."

"Bitch I been told you that you needed to divorce this no good nigga but you didn't want to listen. I did this to prove a point to you."

Mia took a good look at LaShon and saw that she was actually serious, that her reasoning behind it made it ok.

Mia grabbed a handful of LaShon's hair and wrapped it around her fist as she slammed her into the wall.

"You the most pathetic bitch I know. People tried to warn me that you wanted my life but I didn't believe them because I loved your ass like a sister," Mia said as she continuously banged LaShon's head into the wall.

Mia could see tears forming in LaShon's eyes but Mia didn't give a fuck about those crocodile tears.

LaShon reached out to grab Mia but then Mia wrapped her thick hands around LaShon's throat and tried to choke the life out of her.

Seantrel saw the color leaving LaShon's body and ran over to pull Mia off of her. After struggling for a minute Mia finally let LaShon's throat go and she turned her attention to Seantrel whom hands were on her again. That gave LaShon enough time to grab her purse and run out of the house.

Mia lifted her hand to slap Seantrel again but he grabbed her by the wrist to stop her.

"If you don't want this motherfucker broke you will keep your hands to your damn self. I'm only going to warn you once," Seantrel said through clenched teeth.

"I hate you, out of all the bitches in the world you had to pick my motherfucking best friend."

"Man it wasn't even like that just let me explain it to you."

"What the fuck ever, save your explanations for somebody who actually cares now let me go."

Seantrel released Mia's wrist thinking that she was about to spaz out on him again but she didn't even look back his way as she walked out of the living room and grabbed her keys and left the house.

Seantrel stood in the living room pacing back and forth. His devious ways had finally caught up with him and he didn't know what would happen next. Out of all the women that he had been fucking the one time that Mia actually caught him in the act was with her best friend. He knew that it was very careless on his part to even allow things to get so far with LaShon. He never thought that they would get caught though because Mia was supposed to still be at work.

Seantrel had been avoiding LaShon's advances for the last six months. She had been throwing her pussy at him left and right but he wouldn't go that far because of the love that he still had for his wife until a drunken night about a month ago.

Seantrel was at a club with his guys hanging out and was pretty drunk. LaShon just so happened to be at the same club and she were looking good in her mini skirt and low cut blouse. She didn't leave anything for the imagination and Seantrel's blood instantly rushed to his dick.

Seantrel had walked out of the club because he wanted to get as far away from LaShon as he could but she followed right behind him on his heels.

"Seantrel," LaShon called out.

"Damn girl, what do you want," he asked as he got in his car.

"You already know what I want so you need to stop playing and from the looks of things something else wants me too," LaShon said looking down at his hard rod.

Seantrel was about to protest but before he could say another word LaShon had pulled his dick out and was straddling his lap and she fucked him right there in the club parking lot and once Seantrel had bust his nut she got up and left as if nothing had happened. They had hooked up two other times after that but then Seantrel's conscious kicked in and he called their fling off.

LaShon wasn't taking no for an answer that easy so she kept blowing up Seantrel's phone and he ignored her up until today when she showed up at his house with a little bitty shirt on and a little ass pair of shorts talking about they needed to talk about what had happened between them.

LaShon and Seantrel had sat and talked about the situation and before Seantrel knew it he was fucking her again and then made her give him some head and that was when Mia walked in.

Seantrel walked over to the table to get his phone and dialed Mia's phone number. She sent him right to voice mail so he decided to leave a message. He knew that whenever she

142

got mad at him that she would ignore his calls but always checked her voicemail.

Hey baby, please come back home so that we can talk. We can get through this like we do everything else. If you really love me then we can make this work.

Seantrel hit end on his phone and then threw it on the couch. He needed to talk to someone but didn't have anyone to talk to. He was too ashamed of himself to tell anyone what he had done. Everyone warned him over the years that Mia was going to get tired of his shit and leave his ass. He just hoped today wouldn't be the day because he wouldn't know what to do if he had to go without seeing his wife and kids on a daily basis. He loved them more than life itself. He just chose to make dumb decisions with his life.

Seantrel did something that he hadn't done in a while. He got down on his knees and prayed to God that his wife would find a way to forgive him and to not take his family away from him.

CHAPTER 22

LaShon stood in her mirror at home looking at the bruises on her neck pissed off. She never intended on Mia finding out about her and Seantrel so soon but she was glad that Mia finally saw with her own eyes that Seantrel wasn't shit. Granted that she was the one throwing herself at him but he could've fought her off harder.

LaShon kind of understood now what had Mia so hooked on Seantrel though because that man sex game was definitely on point. He could make her toes curl and make her body cum uncontrollably on demand. He did shit to her that no other man was even capable of doing. Seantrel still hadn't given her head yet but she could tell by the way that he licked his lips that the head game was on point too. She knew it was only a matter of time before he did that as well.

LaShon felt no shame in what she was doing. She hated the fact that Mia met Seantrel and moved on with her life without her. Mia had got a new job and moved way across town leaving LaShon at home alone with her mother. It had gotten to the point where Mia had stopped calling her or even going out with her.

LaShon knew that Mia was married with kids and that they would have to be her main priority but she didn't care anything about that.

Mia's life was finally crumbling down and LaShon was ready to take Mia's place and role. She wanted Mia to get a taste of what it felt like to be not wanted and alone. She knew it would only be a matter of time before Mia completely cracked. Mia wasn't cut out to be on her own so she wouldn't have any choice but to go run crying to Mianca.

LaShon had just what it would take to make Mia want to go jump over a bridge. She had just taken a pregnancy test this morning and it came back positive. She was 100% sure that it was Seantrel's because she made sure not to fuck anyone else the month before she slept with him and she hadn't slept with anyone else since she got a taste of him. She wasn't sure if she conceived the first night that they had sex since Seantrel was so drunk that he didn't even put a condom on or if it was the other couple of times that they had sex.

Seantrel always made sure to strap up but she also made sure to prick the condom every time that she put it on him. LaShon wasn't any fool and knew that she had just hit the jackpot because Seantrel wouldn't have any choice but to take care of his child. He could do things the hard way or the easy way. Either way he was coming out of his pockets.

LaShon knew more than likely that Seantrel would deny the baby or tell her to get an abortion if he believed that it was his but there was no way in hell that was going to happen. She had worked to damn hard to get pregnant by him so she wasn't letting up that easily. She had tried the same routine on Mia's ex-boyfriend Dante but he wasn't having it. He made sure to bring his own condoms every time as well as putting it on himself because he didn't trust her.

LaShon lay across her couch with a satisfied smile on her face. Everything was finally going the way that she wanted it to and nothing or no one could take the look of satisfaction on her face away.

CHAPTER 23

Mia drove to the liquor store to grab a bottle of Hennessey and cracked the bottle open before she even walked out of the store. She stood at her car and took a few swigs from the bottle before getting back in her car. She drove around aimlessly without a destination in mind.

Mia's tears blurred her vision so badly that she had to pull over numerous times to keep from crashing into something. She said a silent prayer and asked God to give her strength. She had the slightest clue of what to do or where to go. She was too embarrassed to talk to Mianca about it because Mianca had warned her a while ago to pull the plug on her and LaShon's friendship. Mia remembered the conversation between her and Mianca like it was yesterday.

Mia was lying across Mianca's couch whining about what had been going on in her life.

"Mianca I don't know what to do. I've tried everything with her to mend our friendship and nothing is helping. She's distanced herself from me." Mianca rolled her eyes in her head.

"I told you something is off with that girl. You did what you could now keep it moving. You don't have to kiss her ass."

"You don't get it, that's my best friend; she knows all of my deepest and darkest secrets. I can't just give up on her."

"Do you hear yourself? You are 25 years old now. Some people are only meant to be in your life for a season and LaShon's season over ran her course a while ago baby girl. Open your eyes; she doesn't want to see you happy. She wasn't even there for Sennett's christening.

146

Mia sat there and allowed her sister words to marinate in her head. She never looked at it that way though. She couldn't understand why LaShon wouldn't want to see her happy. Mia had done her best to make sure that LaShon was happy. Mia had even got to the point where she was helping LaShon pay her bills and rent so that she could have extra money to do whatever it was that she wanted to do.

"I guess you are right, I'll cut my ties with her and then when she's ready we can work things out."

"Good, now let's go eat because I'm starving," Mianca said with a laugh.

Mia shook her head to get that memory out of her head. Because the further she thought about it the further pissed off she got. After that conversation she stopped reaching out to LaShon. Mia no longer helped her financially or checked on her to make sure everything was alright with her.

This is all Mianca's fault Mia said to herself. Mia sat in the car for a few more minutes and banged her up against the steering wheel until she started feeling slightly dizzy.

Mia took a few more swallows of her Hennessey before she pulled back out into traffic and headed towards Mianca's house. She looked down at the clock and saw that it was 3:05 P.M. which meant Isaiah was still at work so Mianca would be home alone.

Mia pulled up to Mianca's house and parked the car without bothering to turn the engine off.

Mia walked up to Mianca's door and banged on it like she was the police until Mianca answered the door.

"Why the hell are you banging on this door like you're fucking crazy," Mianca yelled!

"It's your entire fault," Mia slurred as pushed Mianca out of the way almost knocking her over.

Mianca instantly smelled alcohol on Mia's breath and knew nothing good was going to come of her visit.

"Please have a seat and tell me what the hell it is that you're talking about."

"Nooooo," Mia screamed out.

Mianca took a few steps backwards because she wasn't sure what to do. She hadn't seen Mia act out like this since their brother passed away and they had to put her on meds then.

"Mia, just calm down," Mianca said calmly trying her best not to upset Mia any further.

Mia didn't respond Mianca; instead she picked up the lamp from the end table and threw it up against the wall.

"I don't know what the fuck you do at your house but don't you come around here breaking shit."

"My house," Mia said with a laugh. "I don't have a fucking house. That is Seantrel's house. That's the house that I caught my husband and LaShon fucking in."

"Wait, what happened now? When did this happen?" It was all making sense to Mianca now why Mia was acting like she lost her damn mind.

"You heard me and like I stated when I first got here, it's your entire fucking fault bitch."

Mianca looked at Mia like she had just sprouted an extra head. "How is your husband being a hoe and your best friend being an even bigger whore my fault? I didn't raise either one of them." Mianca paused and then continued "don't even bother about answering that question, talk to me when you sober."

Mia wasn't trying to hear anything Mianca was saying. She rushed over to Mianca and knocked her down on the couch. Mia hovered over Mianca and continued to punch her. Mianca had to lift her hands over her face to stop Mia from hitting her there. Mia continued to punch and shake Mianca until she felt a strong pair of arms wrap around waist and pull her off of Mianca.

"What the fuck are you doing?" Isaiah yelled as he tossed Mia across the room so that he could check on his wife.

Isaiah turned back around after Mia didn't reply and he could see the glazed look in her eyes and knew that she was heavily intoxicated. He didn't have time to ask her what was going on because he needed to help Mianca up and check her out.

Mia watched how delicate Isaiah was with Mianca and she instantly felt jealous. She turned around and rushed out of the house and to her car.

"Isaiah go after her, she's been drinking and doesn't need to be driving like that."

Isaiah stood there and hesitated for a second because if it wasn't for Mianca he would let Mia be but he knew he wouldn't hear the end of it.

By the time Isaiah ran outside and made it to the driveway he couldn't spot Mia's car from either angle. He pulled out his phone and tried to call her but she didn't answer him. She allowed the phone to ring twice and then sent him to voicemail.

Isaiah walked back in the house in utter confusion.

"Can you tell me what the hell did I miss while at work?"

Mianca sat there and explained the little bit of information she got from Mia to Isaiah. All Isaiah could do was shake his head. He didn't know who he was more disappointed in LaShon or Seantrel. They had committed the ultimate betrayal and he felt sorry for Mia. He could only imagine how she was feeling right now. He hated that she took it out on Mianca but he also knew that she wasn't in her right mind right now. She could never deal with conflict well.

"So what do you want to do love," asked Isaiah?

"I want to go beat the shit out of LaShon and Seantrel."

"Babe I know but I can't allow you to leave this house and go acting crazy."

"I know and I want I guess we need to just sit tight and hope and pray that Mia is alright and comes back here so that we can get her some help."

Mianca balled up and lay on Isaiah's shoulder and cried gently. Isaiah rocked his wife back and forth. He hated when she was hurting because he felt as if he could feel the same pain that she was feeling and he wasn't too keen on pain. He was going to wait until Mianca was relaxed enough and then he was going to pay Seantrel a visit. He loved Mia like she was his very own little sister and he couldn't let Seantrel to get away with what he had done.

150

CHAPTER 24

Mia drove away from Mianca's house at the speed of lightening towards the lake front. She wanted to turn around and go apologize to her sister but she was too embarrassed by the way that she had just acted. She didn't know what had come over her. It was like she had just blacked out. She felt so alone and afraid that she found no reason to breath the same air as everyone else. In Mia's mind the only person that would care if she lived or not would be her father and he too would get over it like everyone else did when her brother died.

Mia parked her car and broke down and cried. She let out all of the pain that she had been feeling from her mother's resentment, from her brother leaving her alone and from the things that subdued from her relationship with Seantrel.

Mia pulled out her phone and sent Mianca a text. Once she was satisfied she reread it and then pressed send.

I'm sorry for what I did to you. I don't know what came over me but you did not deserve that. I hope you find a way deep down in your heart to forgive me. I just want you to know that I love you.

Mia then generated a group message for Seantrel and LaShon. She figured that she could kill two birds with one stone.

You two were some of the most important people in my life. I would have done anything that you wanted me to. I was always there like I was supposed to be and instead of you two telling me thank you y'all decided to thank yourselves. I hope that you are happy with your decisions and make sure to take care of my babies. Let them know that their mother loved them dearly but life had become too much. Have a nice life.

Mia pressed the send key and then got out of the car and climbed the rocks that overlooked the water. She closed her eyes and decided to do one last prayer.

"Lord please forgive me for what it is that I'm about to do. I don't see another way out and I don't think that I will ever be capable of finding happiness. Lord please watch over-," she started but was interrupted by the vibration of her phone. She looked down at the phone and hit ignore when she saw that it was Seantrel calling her.

Mia closed her eyes to continue her prayer but her phone began to vibrate again immediately. She was about to turn the phone off but then she saw that it was Donovan and decided to answer.

"Hello!"

"Hey baby girl, is everything alright. Something told me that I needed to call and check on you."

"Hmmm, everything's fine," Mia said as she looked around at the body of water in front of her.

Donovan instantly caught on to Mia's voice that something was wrong and he was glad that he followed his gut instinct and called her.

"Everything doesn't sound like its fine. Why don't you come over to my place so that we can talk?"

"I can't do that Donovan."

"Mia where are you?"

Donovan waited for an answer but there was complete silence. He held the phone for an entire minute and all he could hear was the muffled sound of what sounded like Mia was crying.

Donovan hopped up and put on his shoes and grabbed his car keys and headed for his car.

"Come on baby, stop crying and tell me where you are. I will come to you, just let me know that you are alright," Donovan said on the brink of tears himself.

"I'm at my safe place Donovan and I'm scared. I just give up, I can't do this anymore," Mia cried loudly into the phone.

"Baby I been told you that you don't have to deal with him. I will help you find you a place for you and your babies."

"No it's not just that, I can't do life anymore Donovan. I give up; I'm sorry, please forgive me," Mia said before hanging up the phone.

Mia reached inside of her pocket and took out her razor blade. She finished the prayer that she started earlier and then she cut as deep as she could into her left wrist and then repeated the same on right wrist. She allowed the blade to fall from her hand and leaned her head up against the rocks and she felt a long tear fell from her eye. She closed her eyes as she felt her body fade in out of conscious. She just hoped that it wouldn't take her long to leave. She could picture Maurice in her head and she just yearned to hear his voice.

"Mia, Mia, Mia," Donovan yelled into the phone.

Donovan looked down at the phone and realized that Mia had hung up the phone on him. That caused Donovan to panic even more. He was glad that he paid attention when he and Mia talked. He remembered form numerous conversations with Mia that her safe place was the Lake Front so he broke every traffic rule to get there to her. He drove until he found the part where they would go periodically and saw her car.

Donovan let out a sigh of relief and parked his car and got out of it. He was glad that he was able to find her. He climbed the rocks but his heart immediately sped up when he made it to the top of the rocks and found Mia sitting up against them slumped over.

"Mia, Mia, come on baby, wake up." Donovan shook Mia and looked down at her left wrist and found a thick cut with blood flowing at a fast pace. He hurriedly took off his tank top and ripped it down the middle and tied it around her wrist to try and put some pressure on it to slow down the bleeding.

Donovan lifted Mia and carried her to his car so that he could take her to Mercy hospital. He figured he had a better chance of getting her to a hospital on his own then waiting on an ambulance to come and get her through the traffic.

Donovan drove as fast as the traffic permitted him to. He felt Mia's wrist periodically to make sure that she still had a pulse. Her face was losing some of the color but he could still feel a slight pulse and was at least happy about that part but he knew that he needed to hurry if he wanted her to still live.

Donovan pulled up in front of the emergency room where the ambulances park and hopped out and lifted Mia up from the back seat and rushed through the doors.

"I need a doctor now, she's barely breathing," Donovan yelled.

A couple of the nurses and a doctor ran over with a Gurnee and took Mia from Donovan's arms and ran to the back where they could work on her at. Donovan paced the emergency room back and forth. He didn't have Mia's husband number or her sister's number so he had no idea who to call.

Donovan paced the floor for a few more minutes and then remembered that he had LaShon's phone number from when they worked on a school project together a while back. He knew that LaShon had to at least have Mia's sister or father number since her and Mianca had been friends for most of their entire lives. *I guess keeping all of my contacts pays off. I just hope she still has the same phone number*, Donovan thought to himself.

Donovan dialed LaShon's number and prayed that it was still the same number and that she would answer his call. He wasn't sure if she still had his number saved or not.

"Hello," LaShon answered.

"Hey this is Donovan; we use to go to school together. I'm not sure if you remember me or not."

"Of course I remember you, how could I forget a man so fine?" LaShon asked boldly.

Donovan smiled from flattery but he was use to women like this and paid them no attention.

"I'm calling because I need Mia's sister Mianca phone number. Something has happened and Mia is in the hospital."

"Just like this bitch to go and do something to take Seantrel's attention from me and back to her," LaShon said out loud.

"Her phone number is 773-555-5400," LaShon said and hung up.

Donovan looked down at his phone and realized that LaShon had hung up before she allowed him to say thank you and she didn't even show a bit of concern or want to know what happened. Donovan made a mental not to find out later what was going on with Mia and LaShon. He didn't have time to dwell on it now so he dialed Mianca's number. It seemed like the phone had barely rung when Mianca eagerly answered the phone.

"Hello!"

"Hey this is Donovan, a friend of your sister. She's in the hospital."

Before Donovan could finish saying what was going on he heard Mianca crying in the background and then heard a male's voice on the phone.

"Hey this is Mianca's husband, what's going on with my sister?"

Donovan gave Isaiah the information to the hospital and told him that he'd still be there by the time that they got there.

Donovan hung up the phone and sat down in one of the seats in the waiting area. He still couldn't figure out what could have happened so bad that Mia would want to end her life and not be able to spend another minute with her kids. He knew that she loved her kids unconditionally.

Donovan sat in the waiting area lost in his thoughts. He vowed to himself that once Mia got out of the hospital he was going to help her no matter what and there was no way that she was going to stop him.

CHAPTER 25

"I'm not fucking calling him so leave it alone. This is his entire fault anyway. My sister better be alright when I get to that hospital."

"I know that you're upset but that's his wife. Seantrel has the right to know that Mia is in the hospital plus we don't even know if he has the kids yet or even if they are with her."

Mianca and Isaiah had been arguing back and forth since they left the house and headed to the hospital. Mianca saw no reasoning in calling Seantrel because she didn't want to be in the same room as him.

"Well then you are the one who's going to call him and tell him to stay the hell away from me," Mianca said with an attitude.

Isaiah shook his head at his wife as he dialed Seantrel's number. Once Mianca was upset you were basically wasting your breath if you tried to talk to her or even reason with her.

"Have you heard from Mia? Her ass never went and picked up the kids from daycare now I have to go do her job," Seantrel said angrily.

"What the fuck do you mean go do her job? Those are your motherfucking kids too nigga."

Seantrel was taken aback by Isaiah words and the tone of his voice. That let him know automatically that Mia had went crying to them already about what had happened.

"Look, I don't have time for this bullshit. Tell Mia while she out there crying to y'all about our problems she needs to be picking up our kids and bringing her ass home. I would tell her myself but she sent me a dumb ass text message and ain't been answering my calls or replying to my text messages since."

Mianca heard Seantrel through the phone and snatched it from Isaiah.

158

"If your punk ass would shut the fuck up and listen you would know that Mia is at Mercy hospital."

"Hold on say what now?" Seantrel just knew that he had to be hearing Mianca wrong.

"You heard me and no I don't know what's going on with her so if you want to know you need to take your ass up there like I am," Mianca said before hanging up on Seantrel.

Seantrel looked at his phone not believing how Mianca had just spoken to him and then hung up without giving him any details on what was going on with his wife.

Seantrel looked at the time on his phone and saw that he wouldn't have enough time to go pick up the kids and then go to the hospital so he sent LaShon a text asking her to pick up the kids and drop them off at the hospital.

LaShon agreed to pick the kids up so Seantrel headed straight to the hospital. During the drive to the hospital all kind of crazy thoughts were going through Seantrel's head. He just hoped everything was fine with Mia. He couldn't possibly even muster up the right thoughts to know what had happened within those few hours.

Seantrel pulled up to the hospital and parked. He walked inside of the ER and saw Isaiah sitting in the waiting area.

"Where is my wife?"

Isaiah let out a slight chuckle. "It's so funny how you are concerned about your wife's well-being when she's laying up in a hospital bed."

"I don't have time for this shit. Where the fuck is she?"

Isaiah jumped up from his seat but he saw all of the on lookers looking at him so he maintained his composure. "Go to the nurse's desk and she'll let you in the back."

Isaiah sat back down in his seat and watched Seantrel walk away. He couldn't do anything but shake his head at Seantrel.

Seantrel went to the nurses desk like Isaiah instructed and they told him exactly where Mia could be found. But they also informed him that she had two visitors already so one of them would have to leave.

Seantrel walked to the back to where Mia was and walked in the room and had to do a double take. Mianca was sitting on the edge of Mia's bed with her head in her hands but that's not what caught his attention first. The dude sitting on the side of the bed with his head lying on Mia's stomach did.

Seantrel saw how comfortable the man looked laying there and knew that the man had some type of feelings for his wife. That instantly pissed Seantrel off and he was about to say something but the doctor tapped Seantrel on the shoulder so that he could get pass him.

"Hello, my name is Dr. Tompkins the nurses told me that someone needed to speak with me."

"Yes, I'm Mia's sister and that's her husband," Mianca said pointing at Seantrel. Donovan had never opened his eyes or looked up so he never even knew that Seantrel was in the room. He looked up at Seantrel with a look of hate in his eyes.

The doctor looked between Seantrel and Donovan not sure if he should speak or not. He figured that the man who had been by her side since she was brought in was her husband.

Mianca saw the hesitation written over Dr. Tompkins face and spoke up.

"It's alright; please let us know what's going on."

"Well Mia lost a lot of blood from the lacerations on her wrist. It was a good thing that she was brought in when she was. She didn't need a transfusion but she did need stitches in both wrists. We have her sedated right now because we're not exactly sure how she'll react once she wakes up so we want to have her in her private room first. We're going to have to keep her for 72 hours on suicide watch. We'll have a psychiatrist evaluating her and we'll determine what is best for her after that. Do you all have any questions?"

"Why does my wife have to stay in here for 72 hours and why is she strapped down to the bed?"

"Mr. Anderson in suicide cases this is how we have to treat a patient until they are in their own personal room and it takes 72 hours for us to run the proper tests for her."

"My wife is not crazy."

"Man shut your ass up; don't come in screaming that my wife crap. It's partially your fucking fault that she's up in here," Mianca screamed.

"Mianca calm down, you know Mia wouldn't want you in here arguing with this dude," said Donovan.

"Ok, and who the fuck is you? And what the fuck were you doing with Mia."

Donovan looked at Seantrel and didn't bother about responding to him.

"Mianca it's crowded in here so I'm going to the waiting area. Can you please come let me know when they move her to a room?"

"Sure, and thanks for everything Donovan."

Donovan winked at Mianca and then walked out pass Seantrel with a smirk on his face.

Donovan entered the hospital waiting area and saw LaShon sitting down on one side of the waiting area and a man with Mia's kids on the other side of the room.

SJ instantly climbed out of his seat and began to walk over to Donovan.

"Hey little man," Donovan said meeting SJ the rest of the way.

"I apologize, usually he's not this friendly with strangers," said Isaiah.

"Oh, it's cool and I'm not a stranger. I'm friends with Mia; I was the one that talked to you on the phone."

"Oh ok, thanks for looking out for her. We truly appreciate it."

"Damn Donovan, you can't speak," LaShon asked as she stood up from her seat.

"Speak to you for what? I called your ass and you had a messed up attitude and acted like you could care less about what was going on with Mia."

Isaiah looked at LaShon and shook his head. He hadn't had two words with her since she'd brought in his niece and nephew.

"Why are you still here? I'm sure Mia doesn't want to see you right now," said Isaiah.

LaShon had to take a deep breath to keep from saying the first thing that came to mind.

"Seantrel is the reason I'm still here. I need to talk to him."

Donovan looked at both Isaiah and LaShon with a confused look. He had no idea what was going on and he wasn't even sure if he wanted to know.

Isaiah was about to say something but before he could utter a word Seantrel was walking their way with Mianca right on his heels.

"Who the fuck is you and what the fuck was you doing with my wife?"

"I was doing what you should have been doing and who I am is not what's important right now," Donovan said smoothly.

"Man go on somewhere with that bullshit-," Seantrel started but stopped when he saw Mianca walk up to LaShon and smack the shit out of her.

LaShon instantly held the side of her face. "You bitch," LaShon screamed as she reached for Mianca but felt Isaiah grab her away from Mianca.

"Get your fucking hands off of me before I press charges on both of y'all's asses," LaShon screamed out.

"Bitch you lucky all you got was a slap with your disrespectful ass. What the fuck are you even doing here," asked Mianca?

"I'm here because Seantrel asked me to be," LaShon said with a smile.

"Well you and he both can get the fuck out. I'm sure you too are the last people on this earth my sister would want to see anyway. I only called Seantrel because my husband told me too and we needed to make sure someone had my niece and nephew. Now that we have them you two can go," Mianca said loudly.

"Man I don't know who you think you are but that's my wife and I have every right to be here as anyone else does."

Mianca turned to face her attention back at Seantrel but a dark skinned husky security guard walked their way.

"I am only going to tell you all this once. This is a hospital and you all are disturbing other patients. If you guys can't quiet down I will have no choice but to kick all of you out."

"Sorry about that, we'll quiet down" Isaiah said speaking for everyone.

The security guard turned and walked away but made sure not to go too far away from the group.

LaShon walked over to Seantrel and grabbed him by the arm.

"Come on so that we can go. We don't have to deal with this shit."

Seantrel snatched his arm away from LaShon. I'm not going anywhere with you. I have to stay here and make sure everything is alright with Mia."

"So you're choosing her over me again," asked LaShon.

"LaShon you can't be serious right now," asked Donovan?

"Look, you don't have shit to do with this," LaShon said to Donovan and then refocused her attention back to Seantrel.

"So what we have doesn't mean anything to you?"

"LaShon the most we have a few nights of meaningless sex."

Seantrel's words cut LaShon deep like she had just been stabbed with a knife. She really wanted to cry but instead she smirked at him.

"Oh that's what you think? We'll see once your baby gets here."

"What the fuck do you mean when my baby get here?"

"You know what that means but I'll make it a little clearer for you. I'm pregnant, it's yours and I'm keeping it."

Seantrel lunged for LaShon and wrapped his hands around her thin neck. Mianca, Isaiah, and Donovan stood looking in awe as security and a police officer came over and pulled Seantrel off of LaShon.

SJ began to cry causing Mianca to turn around and wrap her arms around him. They had been so caught up in

165

their own world that they forgot all about the kids. She looked over in Sennets's car seat and saw that she was still asleep.

"It's alright man," Mianca said rubbing her nephew's back.

Mianca went and sat down with SJ and watched as the police officer handcuffed Seantrel and led him out of the hospital. She looked at LaShon with a look of disgust as she stood there trying to catch her breath.

"Do you need to see a doctor," asked the security as he was trying to help her up.

"Hell nah I don't need to see a doctor and get your hands off of me."

"LaShon you need to-," Mianca started but was interrupted.

"Shut up talking to me Mianca, I'm out of here. I need to go find out if I can get a bond for Seantrel," said LaShon before she walked out of the visiting room.

CHAPTER 26

"Excuse me, can you tell me what room Mia Anderson has been moved to," asked Mianca?

The receptionist told Mianca the room number and handed her two passes. One pass was for her and the other one for Donovan since he was the one standing next to her.

Donovan and Mianca rode the elevator together quietly not knowing what to say to one another.

Mianca led the way to Mia's room and took a deep breath before walking into the room. A nurse was checking Mia's vitals so she stood to the side until she was finished. Once the nurse walked out Mianca and Donovan went and stood next to Mia's bed side.

"Hey baby girl, you had us scared for a minute," Mianca said as she rubbed the top of Mia's head.

"I know and I am so sorry, I don't understand how I could've gotten so weak and I'm sorry for what I did to you as well. I was embarrassed afterwards and didn't know what to do," Mia said as tears rolled down her face causing Mianca to cry as well. It broke Mianca's heart to see Mia hurting so much emotionally and she knew that there was nothing she could do about it.

"Shhhh, don't even worry about it. The main focus right now is getting you better for those babies of yours."

The mention of Mia kids caused her to cry even harder. *How could I be so stupid* Mia thought to herself?

Mia looked up at Donovan as he wiped her tears away. "I don't know how I could ever thank you enough. I owe you my life. They told me you were the one to bring me in."

"No thank you needed baby, I just hope that you will allow me to help you through this," Donovan said sincerely.

"As bad as I would love for you to rescue me I just can't right now. No one can help me at this point but me. LaShon and Seantrel hurt me to the core, I know I didn't tell you what was going on but I will at a later date. Right now I have to focus on getting better for me my kids. So it pains me to tell both of you that after today I don't want any visitors and all I ask is that you look in from time to time on my babies until I come home Mianca."

Mianca couldn't bring herself to tell Mia what all took place downstairs or that Seantrel was in jail.

"You don't have to worry about the kids Mia, just focus on you sis. They will be in good health when you come home," Mianca spoke honestly. Mia's kids would be in good health because they would be with her for the next few days until Mia came home.

"Mia are you sure that you want to go through this alone," asked Donovan. He wasn't willing to give up without a fight.

"Yes I'm sure Donovan; I have to allow myself to love myself before I can move forward with someone else. I will make sure to call you when I get home though."

Mia saw the sadness in Donovan's eyes and had to turn her head away.

Mianca saw the interaction between Mia and Donovan and she could tell that Donovan cared deeply for her sister.

Mianca leaned down and kissed Mia on the forehead.

"I'm going to give you two some privacy. But just know that I love you baby girl and if you change your mind about the no visitor's I'm only a phone call away."

"I know and I love you for that."

Mia watched Mianca walk out of the room before she turned her head around to face Donovan.

"That is the last thing that I want you to think is that I don't care. I am very grateful for you but I need you to understand that this is what's best for me."

"I know it is Mia, just call it me being selfish. I can't help that I'm falling for you hard."

Mia smiled slightly, had this been any other day Mia's heart probably would have melted at those words and she'd have dropped the draws for him but those days are very far away right now.

Mia was about to say something but the nurse stuck her head into the room. "Sorry but visiting hours are over with on this floor."

"Alright thank you," said Donovan.

Donovan leaned over and kissed Mia softly on the lips without speaking anymore words and exited the hospital room.

Mia watched Donovan walk out. She knew that he was hurt and at one point she saw herself leaving Seantrel to be with him but right now she wasn't too sure of who she wanted to be with. The only thing she was sure of was that she had to figure out how to love her again so that she could her children properly. She knew that there was no way in hell that she could have loved herself if she allowed somebody else's ignorance to make her want to take her own life.

Mia knew that she had a nice journey ahead of her but she was fed up and ready to take the steps to make it to the end. This couldn't be what her life had to resort to. Mia allowed Seantrel to wrap her up in his web but in the end she knew that she would be able to get untangled from it and when that point came he and LaShon would regret ever crossing her. She was about to show them how much of a bitch she could really be.

"If this is what being in love resorts to then fuck this shit," Mia said out loud before closing her eyes.

Mia placed a lock on her heart that day and the only way you could get to the key is if you swam in Lake Michigan to find it.

TO BE CONTINUED……

Author Notes

I am extremely grateful for the opportunities that have been given to me. This is my 4th Published book since being signed. I never thought that I would make it this far. Originally with my first book I only had a dream and an idea but there was something else in store for me.

There was a time when I wanted to throw in the towel and wondered was it all worth it when things didn't go as expected. I eventually reached out and got the right people in my corner to push me and to motivate me to go harder. I say all of that to say. Never give up on your dream or allow someone to say you can't do something. Use their negative energy as the fuel to your fire. Push yourself and if that doesn't work surround yourself with the right people. It takes a lot of work and dedication but in the end it it well worth it. I hope you enjoyed this book as much as I did writing it. I have another series available on amazon as well titled "Infatuated With Love." I love communicating with my readers so feel free to contact me via Facebook, Instagram, email, or twitter.

Facebook: Author Kevina Hopkins

Twitter: @Vina2006

Instagram: caramel_skin_27

Email: khopkins428@gmail.com

CPSIA information can be obtained
at www.ICGtesting.com
Printed in the USA
LVHW030045180821
695508LV00006B/1000

9 781507 588918